C000281423

BABY STEPS

Louise Braithwaite

Copyright © 2022 Louise Braithwaite. All rights reserved.

The characters and events portrayed in this book are fictitious. Any similarity to real persons, living or dead, is coincidental and not intended by the author.

No part of this book may be reproduced, or stored in a retrieval system, or transmitted in any form or by any means, electronic, mechanical, photocopying, recording, or otherwise, without express written permission of the publisher.

Contents

Breaking Point

The boy in the photo is the image of his mother; ash-blonde, with the same angelic features and large, rather innocent blue eyes. A happy memory of a trip to the beach; it's one of her favourites, and still has pride of place on a slightly cluttered mantel.

Ten years on, his still-fair hair is crimped and dyed soot-black. Today, being a Sunday, he's in his scruff – but on a night in town he'd wear leather trousers, frilled shirt and velvet coat, and would go heavy on the eyeliner. Perhaps the main difference is that he's smiling in the photo; but is now stone-faced - hostile, even - while his mother is close to tears.

"Look," she says desperately, as he flings his case into the lobby. "If I really can't talk you out of this, at least let me know you've got there safe. And keep in touch…."

"No," he mutters. "I just need to sort my head out and get away – from *everyone*. Dad can ring when I've arrived."

"Please, son," she sobs "I…"

"I'm going, Mum. Look after yourself."

Wendy

Chapter One

It took days before I finally stopped crying – and even then, the slightest thing seemed to set me off. I'd think I was getting there, and then, from nowhere, my face would be soaked...Perhaps I didn't help myself by looking through those photos, but I had to hold on to *something*.

My favourite is the one from his Christening. July 3rd, 1967, just a few days after his first birthday - blonde, curly, chubby. The later ones are just as cute. There's one where he's 4 or 5, sitting on his tricycle in the back garden - and then, of course, the one on the mantelpiece, of me and him at the beach in Cornwall. Early-to-mid 70s, that would be; '74, I think, because I remember Brian taking the photo, and I'm sure it was our last holiday together, before splitting up.

The one that got me the most was with his school friends, Philip and Peter. We'd gone over to Sherdley Park that day for the St. Helens show, and the three of them had a great time on the fairground rides. Next to Dan, those poor lads looked so scruffy and neglected. Peter was small, plump and painfully shy; Philip tall, loud, a bit mouthy, but with such a big heart. I'm just so sorry how that ended up, and not proud of how I handled it. You know, I always had a feeling that things couldn't be right at home – but instead of listening to my gut, I listened to Alan...

No doubt you'll say I'm biased – and you'd be right! Every mother thinks their own child's perfect; but all I'll say is that I know I got lucky with Dan. Of course, he had his off-days, like they all do – but he had such loving, caring ways, you could never be annoyed with him for long. And to think, I'd been worried about how hard motherhood might be!

He was talking at ten months; walking before he was 1. I rang Brian at work to tell him. The tears were tripping me – I could hardly get my words out!

"Just try and calm down, love," he said gently. "Then take your time and tell me what's wrong."

"There's nothing *wrong*!" I sobbed. "It's Danny – he's just taken his first steps!"

"Jesus!" Brian laughed. "That's brilliant! But you had me going there- I thought it was bad news! What are you like?"

He saw the funny side, back then. It's not that I *meant* to over-react to things – it's just – well, the best way I can explain it is that sometimes, everything seems too *big*. And even if it's good, it feels like too much to cope with. Overwhelmed – that's the word I'm looking for. Brian, to give him his due, was always patient. But it got out of hand, in the end, and I don't blame him for leaving. I think *I'd* have left me, too!

Chapter Two

I've always been that way, ever since I was a kid; even on my infant school reports, it said "nervous disposition". My mum's just the same, and so was my nan – I'm not sure why. Mum once told me that her grandma – Nan's mother – had a tough life; widowed at a young age, lost a couple of babies. Perhaps that's got something to do with it. I'm only guessing, of course, but it would make sense.

You know that saying, "seeds of doubt"? "It planted a seed of doubt in her mind..." I suppose it sounds a bit cliched, but that's *exactly* what it's like; starts out as nothing, a tiny crumb, but ends up as this – well, this enormous *thing*.

What if it rains today? What if it blows a gale? What if it turns into a hurricane? What if it damages the house? Or, what if it gets so bad that one of us is injured – or even killed?

"That should be your new surname," Brian teased. "Wendy Worrif. Worrif this, Worrif that...?"

"And Worrif I punch you in the gob?" I laughed. "You cheeky git!"

Then we'd play-fight, then kiss – then one thing would lead to another...and I'd feel better, at least for a while. But it soon started to take the shine off everything, especially as Dan got a bit older. Days out, holidays, all ruined, because I *couldn't* just sit back and enjoy them – *had* to keep looking for things to be wrong....

We met back in 1964 – almost 21 years ago. We were both 19 and working at the DSS (or just the "dole", as it was then) signing people on. Bri had already been there a couple of weeks when I started, so he showed me around and sat in with me until I was up to speed; and the first thing I noticed about him was his dry humour and kind, patient manner. He put me at ease straightway, and it was this, not his looks, that attracted me – although he was a handsome enough lad, fair-haired, smartly-dressed as they all were back then. Loved the Beatles, as I did-his haircut was a bit like Paul McCartney's, and as Paul was my fave, that had to be a plus! He lived in Knotty Ash, although he'd grown up off Kensington – and his family were what I'd call "salt-of-the-earth". Very Scouse; perhaps a little rough around the edges, but friendly and kind-hearted. Anyway - we started courting soon after we met, and then it all happened pretty quickly. Married at 20; 21 when we had Dan.

I gave up work, once Dan was born, and just as Brian got promotion. We lived with Mum and Dad at first, while we saved for a deposit on a house; it wasn't always easy. My sister, Janice, is three years younger than me, and we've never got on particularly well. She's quite selfish, even now - at 36, and with two kids of her own – so, you can just imagine her at 17!

The "worry-gene" missed *her* out, that's for sure! She just seemed to glide through life, not really thinking of anyone – and she could see how much it upset Mum but didn't seem to care!

She was clever but didn't put the effort in; failed her A-levels a couple of times, because she was too busy partying. We had a huge row about it once, and she called me "as dull as dishwater", because I hadn't done enough of that myself. And perhaps I *should* have done – but I held back, because I knew Mum would be up all night, fretting. That didn't seem to enter Jan's head – and it really wound me up! Not to mention the way she spoke to Mum…

She turned out okay in the end, but it took a while, and a lot of stress for poor Mum and Dad. She passed her exams the third time round, then finally went to Uni – only to drop out after a year, when she got into the hippie thing. Eventually, when she was nearly 30, she did teacher training at Chester College – it was there that she met her husband, Mike. So, yes, she did settle down – but she's still self-centred, and so laid-back she's almost on the floor!

Brian and I had always thought we'd stay in Liverpool – somewhere in West Derby, near to Mum and Dad, especially as Brian's parents were close by too. The prices were quite high, though; it would have taken a good bit longer to have got the deposit together, and after two years, I couldn't take much more of Jan! We hadn't really thought of St. Helens – but when the house in Windle came along, it was too good to miss out on. It was just like the ones we'd looked at near Mum's – a three-bed semi, with a good-size garden, ideal for Dan, and the area was lovely. Just that bit cheaper, being outside the city, and needed some work – Bri got that sorted, although it did take time.

We were there for over six years – and it was a happy time, despite the tensions. The neighbours were great, and Dan, as he grew up, made some good friends. The only thing that bothered me was that he might have an accident playing out. "Try not to wrap him up in cotton-wool," Bri warned - it always ended in a row.

"Look," he said once, "I'm not saying we should let him run wild – but just try and get more of a balance. He'll end up a bag of nerves, otherwise."

"Like me, you mean?" I snapped back. "And we wouldn't want *that*, would we?"

And I suppose the more it happened, it wore us down. Eventually, when Dan was 8, Brian said we needed to talk. He'd been offered another promotion, which meant a transfer to a different department and a move down south, and he was going – alone. He still cared for me, and of course he loved Dan to bits – but he'd had enough. He knew I couldn't help how I got, but it was draining the life out of him. He'd thought long and hard about it, and it wasn't an easy decision, he said – it would kill him to leave Dan, but the constant arguments were even worse. He'd make sure he stayed in regular contact, and that we were alright for money (and good enough, he always kept his word); but there'd be no going back.

Chapter Three

Of course, I was heartbroken – but not entirely surprised. I'd always known he'd get fed-up I'd always known he'd get fed-up of me, because – well, I got on my *own* nerves at times….! At least it was amicable, which was all the better for Dan; no-one else was involved. It wasn't till a few years later that Brian met his second wife, Sue, and we've always been friends - she's a lovely woman.

Having to sell up was the hardest thing. Brian was generous with the divorce settlement, and he gave me most of the proceeds – but still, there was no chance of getting a mortgage on my own. I'd not worked for years and, I'll be honest, the thought of it terrified me; and besides anything else, it would have to be something part-time, to fit around Dan.

Mum and Dad asked me if I'd like to live back with them, but it wouldn't have worked – at least not in the long-term. It might have been different if Jan wasn't there, but it would be a few years before she left to marry Mike; and no good would come of having us under the same roof again, especially now I had Dan to think of. The only other choice would be to rent - so I got my name on the housing list as soon as I could. There wasn't much the council could do much for me, until the house was actually sold – but I let them know once it all went through, and they found me somewhere, much quicker than expected; almost straightaway.

"Well, of course they would," Jan remarked. "They put lone parents at the top of the list."

"Thanks for the reminder!" I snapped; tact was never her strong point.

I went to take a look, and it was just what we needed. Bright, modern, nicely decorated – much smaller than we were used to, but that was no bad thing, as it would save me a fortune on the bills. The back garden was tiny, but at least Dan still had *some* space to play out, and it was just a short bus ride to Sherdley Park - we could work around it. It was just a shame about the dodgy neighbours – and Dan having to change schools.

My friend Jean looked worried. "A council estate?"

"Yes," I said lightly, "but it's really nice – and there's good and bad everywhere."

"I know,'" she said, "but – well, I don't mean to sound snobby, but just be careful."

I knew she meant well, but it seemed unfair, the way council estates were judged – always this implication that it must be somewhere awful. "He did well for himself – despite being brought up on a tough council estate…" I lived in Norris Green until I was 7. It gets a terrible name, these days. But back then – late 40's, early 50's – it was *nothing* like that; not even close! At least not where we were, anyway….

Dad was an electrician, and most of the families were just like ours – stay-at-home mums, and fathers with good, solid trades, all saving to buy homes of their own. Next door were our best mates, Joe and Val Parker – their dad (also called Joe) ran his own business as a builder. Across the road was our other pal, Terence O'Rourke; "Wee Terence," as his mother called him. Never Terry – always got his full title!

Terence was the youngest in his family, by 12 years. His mum, Ada, was in her 40s when she had him – and his father had sadly died when he was a baby. Although Ada was quite a bit older than my mum, they became good friends; this, despite Ada being a devout Catholic, and Mum growing up off Netherfield Road, staunch Orange Lodge! Originally from Glasgow, Ada was from a family she described as "poor, but aspiring", and her father was a self-educated man. She was a clever woman, who had trained as a teacher before her marriage, and returned to it after she was widowed. Mum always kept in touch with her - and by all accounts, Wee Terence had dropped out of college, and had turned out a bit wild. Interesting to think what would have happened if we'd stayed living there; he'd probably have ended up with Jan!

We moved to West Derby around 1952, and the memories soon became hazy - but always good.

Anyway…. Of course, I knew that where we were going would be very different from Windle; but I suppose part of me was hoping it might just be a *bit* like where I'd grown up. And, in fairness, there were some lovely people, who were in the same boat as me, and just trying to make the best of things. But as for the others – well, I can cope with it if someone's a bit rough-

and-ready, if they're friendly with it, but this lot were cliquey; and I got the feeling you'd need to have lived there all your life to be accepted. It was just an attitude – completely blanking me if I let on to them, and this cold, almost hostile manner. I decided the best thing was to keep to myself, and that did work; but I can't pretend it wasn't disappointing.

Then there was the problem with Dan's school; the thing that really made me doubt myself. I felt so stupid for not looking into it more, because although we were moving out of the catchment area, it just hadn't crossed my mind that they wouldn't let him stay. The new house was on the opposite side of St. Helens, but he was so happy and settled at the school that this wouldn't have been an issue; I'd have gladly gone back and forth with him on the bus. But they wouldn't allow it – and I had to find somewhere nearby on the estate.

Chapter Four

I dreaded telling him. I'd expected tears, but he just went quiet; almost no reaction at all. He was even quieter once he'd started – and as each day passed, seemed more and more withdrawn.

"How do you like it?" I asked.

He shrugged. "It's okay…"

"Have you made friends?"

"Yeah."

"Are the teachers nice?"

"Yeah."

"And…look, son – you would tell me if anything was wrong, wouldn't you?"

"Yeah."

"Like, if you were being bullied?"

"Yeah."

"You're *not* being bullied, are you, love?"

At last, a change – "No."

Of course, I knew he was keeping things from me, but what could I do? I couldn't *force* him to tell me! He came home with bruises a couple of times, but said he'd fallen over, or got knocked playing football; and when I picked him up from school, he was always alone.

"You'll have to introduce me to your new friends," I said once.

"Okay," he nodded – but it never happened; and then, a few days later, he said he'd be fine to go to school on his own – he knew I was busy.

"Oh, love," I sighed, "I'm never too busy for you! But listen – if you'd rather I *didn't* meet your friends, don't worry. Just whenever you're ready."

He'd always been slightly on the shy side, but it hadn't mattered while we were in Windle – he was quite content with his own little circle, and was always happy and well-balanced. But now…well, you just *know* when your child's not right, don't you? For a while, I was furious with Brian for leaving – then at myself, for driving him away. If I'd *only* managed to get a better grip on things, we might have stayed together, and we wouldn't be in this mess! And then it crossed my mind – perhaps it was nothing to do with school, and Dan was just missing his dad.

"Has he mentioned anything to you?" I asked Brian on the phone. "Because he's not himself, that's for sure. I've never seen him looking so down!"

"Well," Brian said, "whenever I ask him if everything's alright, he always says he's fine. And I can tell he isn't – but look, Wend, we can't keep pressuring him to open up – he'll just go even further into himself."

"So, what am I supposed to do? I can't just *leave* it!"

"I know that…but listen, I'll try and make sure I visit as much as I can. So he knows I want to be there – and that I wasn't getting away from *him*."

"No – only me."

"Aw, Wend, come on, I didn't mean…"

"It's okay, Bri – I know it's true."

Maybe it was school, or maybe Brian – most likely a bit of both. All I know is that I was more than relieved when he brought Philip and Peter back for tea; and seemed to get back something of himself.

They didn't have a dad; only a mum, but they never mentioned her, as far as I recall. They often talked about their grandparents – or at least Philip did; Peter said very little, but his eyes would light up when the food arrived.…

They both had enormous appetites and would gobble up everything I put in front of them, with seconds and even thirds! Philip was tall, thin and a bundle of energy, while Peter, being much shorter, was inclined to gain weight, and I got the feeling he was eating for comfort. From what I could gather, they'd lived with their grandparents till quite recently, and Philip often remarked fondly that my dinners were like his nan's. I could tell straightaway that they just ate junk-food at home and wouldn't have got decent meals – or much of anything else.

I felt terrible for saying this, but to me, they always seemed a bit scruffy, even unkempt – and often not very clean. It wasn't *their* fault, God love them, but that mother of theirs, sending them out like that…Then I'd wonder if I was misjudging the woman; she could be sick, or depressed, or just very poor.

It crossed my mind a few times to go to social services – but, I'll be honest, I was terrified of being wrong, or that it would all backfire. It might turn out that their mum really loved them but, for whatever reason, wasn't coping; and imagine her heartache if, instead of being given the help she needed, her sons were taken away! And if my first hunch was right, and she truly was a bad, uncaring mother? The hope would be that they'd be placed back with the grandparents – but I knew nothing about them, and if they were deemed too old or ill to manage, the boys could end up in care. I'd heard some bad things about children's homes – how true, I'm not sure – but even so, I had to ask myself if they'd really be better off?

Instead, I tried to find out as much as I could about the grandparents, in the hope I might be able to get in touch. They were from Sutton Manor, Philip told me – and their grandad had been a miner before he retired.

"Did you live near Jubits Lane?" I asked - I knew that was the main road to the colliery.

"Yeah," he said. "Just off there. Tennyson Street."

Much later, once Dan was in bed, I called directory enquiries. But no luck; they must have been ex-directory, or maybe not on the phone at all. The best I could do was keep a close eye on things – and if I sensed it was getting worse, just come straight out and ask the boys if they wanted me to speak to their nan.

Chapter Five

It was around this time that I met Alan – through a dating-agency, which I'd joined a few months earlier, despite my friends' best attempts to talk me out of it.

"Just watch yourself," Jean said. "Our Brenda did the same thing, after Tom died. Not for long, though – she said there were too many weirdos."

"Well," I joked, "I'm a weirdo myself, so I'll be in good company!"

But, in all seriousness, I could see where Jean was coming from. Her sister, Brenda, had met some very dodgy characters – and when she finally found someone who seemed okay, he turned out to be on the make. But poor Brenda was lonely and vulnerable, completely lost after being widowed so young; and although I still missed Brian, what I'd been though didn't come close. And besides anything, how else would I ever meet someone? I'd never been one for night-clubs - but even if I was, it was out of the question with Dan.

Of course, I asked myself many a time if I *needed* to meet anyone at all – and for Dan's sake, as much as my own, I thought I did. The money side of things played a big part, and I'll always be upfront about that. Before anyone starts judging, all I'll say is that I was lonely, and never settled on that estate - and raising a child on your own is hard enough as it is. Although Brian did his best, and made sure we never went under, I still had to watch every penny, and …don't get me wrong, I knew some had it much worse than us, but I wanted something more for my son; was that so awful?

Apart from that, I didn't think it would do any harm for Dan to have a father-figure. Because Brian was living away, he only got to see him once a month. They did speak regularly on the phone, but Dan was growing up fast - and I just felt it wasn't quite enough.

There were a few duds before Alan – and when he came along, I could hardly believe my luck. Tall, muscular, chiseled, with his thick moustache and shock of jet-black hair. Very sharply-dressed; a deep, authoritative voice – well-spoken, but with just that hint of Scouse to add some warmth. But what attracted me more than anything was his *confidence*. If just a *drop* of it could rub off on me, perhaps I'd finally stop second-guessing myself.…

He was a year or so older than me, and the Head of Finance for an insurance firm. Very driven, which was a real change from steady-eddy Brian; I know Bri was doing well, but he was the first to admit he was a "plodder", and not competitive at all. Alan, on the other hand, believed nothing was worth doing if you weren't the best. Like climbing Everest, he said – you only heard of the ones who reached the summit, not the ones who'd only got midway. It never crossed his mind that he *couldn't* do something, and I thought this might help to balance me out. Bri had often said I didn't listen when he tried to calm my nerves – and I think that was because he might *say* things would work out fine, but never sounded totally *sure*. With Alan, there was never any doubt – always that firmness, that certainty; and in those early days, it made me feel safe.

He had a company car and lived in Liverpool, a shortish drive from Mum and Dad. It was a large, detached house on Menlove Avenue, in a leafy setting near Calderstones Park - too big for someone on their own, he said. He'd been thinking of downsizing, but that would change, of course, if he met someone to settle down with…He'd been divorced for three years, and spoke little about his ex-wife, except that she had "mental problems" and was "very unstable." He'd had a few girlfriends since then, but none of them had worked out, as they'd all had their "issues" too.

When I look back, perhaps *that* was the first red flag. My immediate thought was how sorry I was that he'd been through such a rough time – and that I'd try to get a handle on my own anxieties, so I could make him happy, and not mess things up like I'd done with Brian. Yet somewhere, at the back of my mind, I made a note to myself that I'd best not mention it to Mum. It might put him in a bad light with her, because she'd warned me to beware "when it's always everyone else – never *them.*"

We did have some good times; perhaps that's why I chose not to see it. Our favourite haunts were the Berni Inn, the Mariners' Steakhouse and the Golden Phoenix. It was usually on a Friday, and he'd pick me up around 6 from Mum's; I'd take Dan there straight from school, and she'd give him his dinner while we were out. He always looked forward to it – he thinks the world of his nan and grandad, and kept up the Friday night tradition well into his teens, long after Alan had gone.

Alan would pop in for a coffee and a chat with Mum and Dad when we got back, and they got on well enough with him- or at least they seemed to. It came out much later that they'd always sensed *something* not quite right but couldn't put their finger on it. Dad especially had his doubts, but Mum stopped him saying anything, in case I thought they were interfering. She felt awful about it, but she was probably right!

But if I'd had any clue how it would turn out for Dan, I wouldn't have gone near. The trouble was, they really took to each other at first, and that convinced me even more that I'd made the right choice. Straightaway, Alan showed a real interest in him; noticed how clever he was, and said he was a son to be proud of. Just needed a little more confidence, perhaps, but *he'd* sort that out – and true to his word, he gave nothing but help and encouragement. I could see a big difference, even after a month.

"As long as he doesn't think he *has* to change," Brian once remarked.

"Of course not!" I snapped. "Why on earth would you say a thing like that?"

"Look, don't take me the wrong way, Wend. It's great he's doing so well – we just don't want him under any pressure, that's all I'm saying."

Was Brian feeling pushed out? I wondered – or maybe a tad jealous? Well, he'd just have to lump it; it was *him* who left *us*, after all!

Chapter Six

We were in the Tower Restaurant when Alan proposed. It was on my 30th birthday, and he'd bought me the most stunning engagement ring - white gold, with emerald and diamonds. Of course, I grabbed the chance with both hands; there was no reason not to!

I could tell Mum and Dad were a bit shocked at how quick it was – after all, it was only three months since we'd first got together! But they could see how happy I was and wished us all the best. Jan was more critical. "Life doesn't end if you haven't got a man, you know," she said snarkily. I took no notice; that was Jan all over.

I *did* miss being with a man, I'll admit that; a man's touch; a man's desire. Life just seemed better with these things – and without them, it felt like I was just kind of muddling through, instead of really *being*….

Brian had been a patient, gentle lover – perhaps not the most exciting – but it was always good. But Alan took it up a gear – well, several gears, if I'm honest! He was intense, fiery and very dominant, and that was a huge turn-on. Mostly, I enjoyed it when things got a bit rough, seeing it as all part of the thrill. There were a few times, though, when it went a bit *too* far – but that, I told myself, came with the territory of being with such a virile man.

The thing that worried me most was how Dan would react to another big change, in such a short space of time. To my relief, he seemed to take it all in his stride – although I didn't say too much at first about how we'd be moving again. I'd work towards that gradually, I thought; get him used to the idea – in the hope that being nearer to his nan and grandad might compensate for leaving Philip and Peter.

It just crept up on me, I suppose – the amount of time they were spending at our house. It was meant to be once a week, but soon it was nearly every night, and I couldn't help but notice that they always turned up at mealtimes. Of course, I was more than glad that Dan had such good friends – but it really was getting too much. My food bills had started to soar, but that wasn't my only problem; the longer it went on, the harder it would be for Dan when it came time to leave.

I tried to ask them, as nicely as I could, not to come on a Friday, as that was the night Dan saw his nan and grandad. "Okay," Philip nodded; but when they turned up anyway, I had to be more direct. I could see the hurt on their faces, and I felt terrible for that; but, as Alan had told me, I *had* to stop putting everyone else first….

"If only it were that easy," I said.

"Of course it is – mind over matter," he replied briskly – perhaps a little *too* briskly, but I brushed that aside, telling myself he was just trying to teach me to be more confident - like he was with Dan.

Anyway, the lads didn't come round for a few days after that, and I was starting to worry. I don't know – perhaps I *was* being a bit too soft, but that was always what bothered me. That by being so "straight-to-the-point" and "telling someone how it is," I'd run the risk of them backing off completely – and in the case of those boys, that was definitely *not* what I wanted! They'd been so good for Dan– but apart from that, there was the concern about what might be going on for them at home. To be honest, there was a big part of me that dreaded how things would be for them once we moved, and hoped we could find some way of staying in touch; although somehow, I had an inkling that Alan wouldn't like that, and might think they weren't suitable friends for Dan. Looking back, there were so many of these tiny doubts, which were so easy to dismiss because, on their own, they seemed like nothing; if I could *only* have taken a step back, and thought about how they added up….

So, it was a relief when they came back the following Wednesday. They seemed a bit subdued, but I made a fuss of them, telling them how good it was to see them, and that cheered them up. For a while, it was nowhere near as much as before -and although it did start to creep up again, it was never on a Friday, which I appreciated. If I hadn't bumped into them with their mother, it would have turned out completely different. Quite honestly, I'm not sure how easy it would have been to keep the friendship going after we'd left, but at least it would have ended on better terms.

I was out shopping on my own – if I remember rightly, I think Dan was at Chester Zoo for the day with his nan and grandad. I only saw them when Philip shouted over- and at first, I thought they were on their own, until I noticed *her*, browsing through the magazines. I'm not sure what I expected, really – all I knew was that she was nothing like it. In my mind's eye, I pictured someone vulnerable- maybe ill – certainly not someone well-dressed and well-kempt. Don't get me wrong, she did look – well, I know I must sound like a snob, but what Mum calls "tarty", with her very short hot-pants and lowcut halter-neck top. But clean and tidy – nice hair, perfume, lots of make-up. Pretty and petite – I could see Peter was the image of her (Philip not so much). A few years younger than me – mid-20's at most, so she couldn't have been much more than 16 when they were born.

Of course, all this should have made me *more* worried for them – because if a woman could spend that much time and money on her appearance, but send her sons out, quite frankly looking like tramps…! If she *had* been ill, there'd have been an excuse - and maybe something to work with. But she wasn't sick – just selfish; and by that, I don't mean silly and self-absorbed, like Jan. I mean properly, horribly *selfish*.

Those boys were more at risk with *that* heartless cow than they'd have ever been with the fragile victim I'd imagined. Even now, I beat myself up for not seeing that – and I think the *attitude* of the woman got in the way. Like quite a few around there, she gave me a shitty look when I tried to introduce myself. I thought, naively, that this might change when she realized who I was, but she just sort of *smirked* – and that made me see red. Alan's right, I thought – I *am* too nice; and now here she is, laughing in my face…No doubt *that* was why she could afford to doll herself up – she must have seen me coming a mile off!

"Unbelievable!" I said later to Alan, over the phone.

"Well," he replied, in that dry, matter-of-fact tone he always had when he thought I was being wishy-washy. "I've told you my opinion, Wendy. You should put a stop to it, once and for all."

"But they're only kids, Alan – and it's not *their* fault she's a hard-faced bitch."

"Ah - but that's what these people *play* on, you see! And those boys are *not* your problem, darling. You need to start being firmer."

Like so much else, it didn't quite sit well with me – but because there was at least *some* element of truth in what he said, it was difficult to argue. Whatever the issue, he'd always be just that little bit right on *something*…Still, the last thing I wanted to do was make life difficult for Dan, so I reached a compromise.

"Look," I told him, "I don't mind if it's a Wednesday, like we agreed. But it can't carry on the way it is. It's getting to be all the time."

Dan looked sad, but didn't seem to protest; perhaps he'd already worked out that things were about to change, and we wouldn't be there much longer anyway. But he did say he knew why they turned up so often – they hated it at home, and their mum sounded horrible.

"Oh, I can believe that, love," I said. "To be honest, I met her the other day and, well – I just get the idea she's making a fool of me."

Whether he really understood what I meant, I can't be sure – but he just nodded, and I thought it would be fine. And perhaps it *might* have been, if not for Philip's reaction. Of course, I knew he was hurt, and disappointed, and was just lashing out, but still – I wasn't going to have my son upset like that. We'd been nothing but kind to them both, and I didn't think either of us deserved it. To be fair to Philip, he did apologize straightaway, and it seemed genuine; but by then I'd had just about enough, and I told them they weren't welcome back.

Poor Dan was in tears for a good while after that. I kept reassuring him that all would be okay – we'd have a new life to look forward to, soon. Different school; better friends. Once he'd calmed down, he seemed to move on quite quickly – or so I thought.

Chapter Seven

We moved in with Alan a few months later, and I married him just before Christmas. Dan settled well at his new school, and once more I saw the happy, balanced kid he'd been when we were in Windle. That in itself made everything worthwhile

The house was stunning – beautiful – and Alan had done all the work on it himself. As well as being so astute with figures, he was a skilled craftsman, which he'd got from his father – a stonemason, and another driven man who was at the top of his game. His family were similar to mine – what I'd call "better-off" working-class (or "aspiring", as Mrs. O'Rourke would call it) – and he'd grown up in Garston, as had both his parents. His paternal grandparents, though, were from the village of Gairloch in the Wester Ross region of the Scottish Highlands – the last in a long line of tough and fiercely hard-working crofters. He once showed me an old photo of his great-grandparents – I could see him clearly in them, and both husband and wife looked rugged, weather-beaten and very severe.

We were happy together at first. I know now, of course, that I was completely in his thrall, but it was real at the time – or at least *felt* real. Not that it was in any way easy – but I didn't *expect* it to be with a man like Alan. Headstrong, demanding, exacting – *his* way or the highway – but then, wasn't that the attraction? After all, I'd *wanted* a strong man, who knew what he needed from a woman, and that's what I'd got – and to begin with I was excited, even thrilled by it. I wasn't *looking* for easy – I'd had that with Brian, and look how that turned out! What I craved was someone I could learn from, who'd challenge me and push me to my limits – or maybe even beyond them.

I'll admit that I waited on him hand and foot. He expected the house to be kept immaculate; meals cooked from scratch, with a whisky chaser to follow, made exactly how he liked; clothes washed, pressed and folded in a particular way, and laid out for him each morning. And before anyone passes comment, *I know*! He was a chauvinistic pig, and I was a weak, *stupid* doormat! When I think of those times, I can hardly believe what a fool I was – but I threw myself into it and put every bit of effort into being the best I could. It's hard to explain, really – but I'd always struggled so much with self-esteem, and when things were good, he made me feel fantastic.

For a start, the sex was bloody amazing! He put huge demands on me in the bedroom, as with everything else, but I loved every minute, back then… The faster, deeper, rougher the better; I might be sore as hell next day, but God, was it worth it!

The other thing was that he worked hard – *really* hard – for the lifestyle we had, and it was fantastic; holidays, meals, no end of gifts; whatever his faults, I could never doubt his generosity. And when I thought of that, I'd have to ask myself if what he expected of me was so much? Yes, he did have high standards, but when I got it right, he'd praise me to the hilt; and for someone who'd doubted themselves as much as I had, that felt pretty damn good! The trouble was, no-one could get it completely right *every* time – not even *him*.

Sometimes, when I think about what went wrong, I wonder if it might have been different if we'd had a child of our own. It wasn't for the want of trying! I know that's sometimes just how it happens, but he had no children from his first marriage, and - well, if it *was* anyone, it was going to be him. The irony couldn't have been lost on him, that mild-mannered, super-laidback Brian had got me pregnant almost straightaway…No doubt this would hurt his ego, and perhaps it made him resent *all* of us – me, Dan, and especially Brian.

He had a pretty low opinion of Brian, and I'll admit, a lot of that was my fault; deep down, I suppose I was still a little sore at Brian for leaving and might have put him in a less flattering light than I needed to. At the time, of course, I had no idea of anything Alan was saying to Dan; but I'm pretty sure that jealousy of Brian was behind it. Because I couldn't help but notice that those barbed comments aimed at me, would seem that tiny bit worse while Dan was away at his dad's - and he always seemed in a bad mood on the lead-up to him going.

A child might have softened him – who knows? But on the other hand, he might have bullied them, too.

Chapter Eight

It took a couple of years to wear me down completely. To begin with, the remarks were small and seemingly harmless – but always *just* enough to make me wonder if I'd failed or let him down in some way. But then, before I'd really had time to think about it, he'd switch back to kind and loving, and showering me with compliments; and that night, in bed, would be better than ever! So, then I'd ask myself what was *wrong* with me, to keep having these doubts about my man? Perhaps, like his first wife, I was a bit unstable....

But it wasn't just the comments – it was those sudden cold snaps, which always seemed to happen just when I needed his support. Like when Dad took ill that time. Thankfully, all turned out okay, but it was still a real shock; Dad was still only in his 50s, and always in great health. I was quite shaken-up by it, and so was Dan. He was only 11, God love him, and his Grandad was his hero – still is! And as it was his first experience of anything like this, it was bound to be scary....

It was a Friday morning when Jan called me to say Dad had collapsed and been rushed to hospital. I could hear Mum sobbing in the background, and to give Jan her due, she did her best to quieten her down. Alan was at work, and Dan at school. I'm not sure why I knocked next-door, when I could easily have called a cab – probably just not thinking straight. Anyway, our neighbour, Betsy Markus, came bustling to the door. A no-nonsense, retired GP, she had a straight-talking manner that

Alan, no doubt, would have admired in another man – but he called her a battle-axe. I'd only spoken to her a handful of times – but I could tell she was kind underneath.

"What *is* it, dear?" she blustered. "You'll have to be quick – I'm about to go shopping!"

"I'm so sorry, Mrs. Markus." (*Dr!* I should have remembered that!). "My dad's in hospital…"

She softened at once. "Well, come on, my love – no time to waste!"

"He's in intensive care," Jan said when I got there – probably the most serious I've ever seen her. "His heart stopped. One of the ambulance guys gave him mouth-to-mouth – he managed to get him back, but he was down for a good ten minutes…."

Mum was crying too much to speak. We just sat, trying to console her, for what I think was about an hour – we lost track of time, but I know it seemed much more, and the longer it went on, the more hopeless it seemed. But then, tears of relief when the surgeon finally came out– "Good news, Mrs. Sinclair. Your husband had a close shave, but luckily, there doesn't seem to be any sign of brain damage. We'll have to monitor him closely, though - it's very early days…."

As expected, Dad was weak and very drowsy; but at least he was awake and knew who we were. I stayed for three, maybe four hours, during which he was drifting in and out of sleep, then I had to leave in time for Dan getting in from school. I wasn't going to say anything to him at first, but he's such a sensitive soul; always knows when something isn't right.

"You've been crying, Mum."

"I know, son," I said. "But it's all fine now."

"What's happened?"

And then, I thought, probably best to be honest; Mum or Jan would probably blurt it out when we saw them. Besides which, he was bound to ask why he wasn't going to his nan's later.... But as I started to tell him, I felt myself tearing up again, and I think it set him off – that and the shock. He cried for a good ten minutes, inconsolably.

"Grandad's okay, you know," I said, once he'd calmed down. "It'll take a while to get him back on his feet, but he's in good hands."

This seemed to comfort him a little – but he was still very subdued. He asked if he could visit his grandad in hospital. Maybe tomorrow, I started to say, and then I caught a glimpse of the time – just gone 5. Alan would be back in less than an hour, and I still hadn't thought about dinner....

Despite being so behind, I managed to rustle something up, and get a bath run for him when he stormed in at 6, as ever in a whirlwind of stress – he was always fairly tense and wound-up when he got home, but even more so this evening, after what he described as an "especially difficult meeting." All things considered, I think I'd done well to catch up; but as he headed to the bathroom, I could tell from his expression that he'd noticed the house was less tidy than usual, and he wasn't best pleased.

I'd cooked sausage and mash for tea. It was quick and easy; something I'd made many a time when I was with Brian, and there was never a problem – but then Brian was so easy-going anyway…It was one of Dan's favourites – he'd asked me a couple of time lately when we'd be having it again – and Philip and Peter had loved it. In fact, as I served it up, it made me suddenly think of them and wonder how they were doing, and that upset me too.

Still, I brushed the tears aside as I brought the plates in. Alan looked at it in horror – I might as well have put a plate of dogshit in front of him! Of course, I'd never made anything like this for him before – it was always something much more elaborate – but even so…! I could almost have laughed at his shocked reaction; then, catching sight of our tear-stained faces, "What on earth's going on?" he asked.

"Dad collapsed today," I said – and as soon as the words were out of my mouth, I knew I was going to cry again. "I was at the hospital. His heart stopped for a while."

"I see." He took a tentative mouthful – then a couple more; perhaps it was better than he'd thought. "So, he's okay now, I take it?"

"Well, yes, but it was such a shock – and…"

"So," he repeated, "he's okay now?"

"Yes."

"Right. Because I'm just struggling a bit to understand exactly what the *problem* is, here?"

"I…well," I stammered, "I…. as I said, Alan, it was just the shock – I mean, Dad's never been ill in his life, and - I don't know, I was just scared I'd lose him."

"But you didn't – did you?"

"No…but…"

"So, there's no problem – is there?"

"No… it's just..." I was about to say that Dad would have a long road ahead of him –time to recover properly, and perhaps more treatment, if they though it could happen again. But I thought twice, for fear of upsetting Dan. "No…. no problem …."

"Good!" Alan laughed. "So, all's well that ends well, eh? Now – I'm just about ready for a drink."

Dan, by now, had finished his dinner.

"Time for homework, Mister," I told him. "And then an early night, I think. It's been a tough day."

"Okay," he nodded, and trotted off upstairs; never a moment's trouble. Once he'd gone up, I started clearing the table – still reeling, and not quite able to believe what Alan had just said.

I know everyone's different – and *no-one* could be more different than Alan and Brian! And no, Brian isn't perfect by any means. Nor am I – nor is anyone! I'd say Brian's main fault, and the thing that got me so wound up, is that there's never any sense of *urgency* with him. Just taking his own sweet time…there's no rush, love…I'll do it later…. Dilatory, my mum once called him – not in a nasty way. "Brian's a lovely fella," she said, "but he *is* a bit dilatory." I couldn't disagree!

But, dilatory or not, I missed Brian so much in that moment, and would have given anything for just a *tiny* bit of his kindness. One thing for sure, if *he* was here with me right now, he'd be holding me until I'd cried it out. No judgement – just there, like you're supposed to be….

Alan followed me to the kitchen – stood watching in silence for a moment as I started washing up.

"I'm still waiting for that drink," he said at last. "You seem to be falling down on the job today."

"I know," I sighed, the tears welling up again, "but please, Alan, just cut me a bit of slack. My Dad nearly died!"

"Yes – and he's perfectly *fine*, now! Look, Wendy, I don't mean this to sound unkind, but you really need to control your emotions better, and stop turning everything into such a *drama*."

"Sorry," I sobbed, "but I can't help loving my dad!"

"No-one's asking you to!" He sounded exasperated. "But, just for a moment, try and look at it rationally. He was ill, but they sorted it out. He *nearly* died, but he didn't. Why be upset about what *didn't* happen?"

"I don't know," I muttered. What was the point?

"Look, the thing is, my darling," he continued, "I know I'm dropping this on you at the last minute, but I've invited Fred Foxton and his wife over for dinner tomorrow – it came out of that meeting I had earlier. He's on the board for that promotion I'm in line for– so, you'll appreciate how important it is. Now, Fred's wife is a fantastic cook, so I really need you to pull all the stops out and deliver. You'll have to put an end to all this sitting around crying, and focus on the task in hand – you do understand me, darling?"

"Yes," I said flatly. "That's fine."

"Glad to hear it. Now – how about that whisky?"

"I'll sort it now."

He smiled. "Good girl."

In bed later that night, I didn't enjoy it as much as usual – in fact, if I'm honest, I can't say liked it much at all! Try as I might, I couldn't relax in his arms, and I was as dry as sandpaper when he went inside me – it hurt like hell.

The meal with Fred went well the next evening – the food was to everyone's liking, and I smiled through it, privately detesting every minute like I always did with Alan's colleagues. I used to get the feeling they were comparing how good their wives were in the kitchen – and possibly the bedroom, too. Fred was a pompous old windbag – well, probably *not* that old, really, maybe my dad's age, but he looked at least 70. His wife seemed very stuck-up. I can't recall her name, but I thought of her as "Hattie"; I'm not sure why.

Dad was in hospital a few more weeks, and they decided to fit a pacemaker. He had to take it easy for a few months (which, safe to say, he hated!), but eventually made a good recovery. Alan did get the promotion he was hoping for, so it all ended fine. But it was never quite the same after that – and I'm not saying I *never* enjoyed sex with him again, but as the put-downs and belittlement increased, I soon began to dread it.

Chapter Nine

Now, I'll be fair here – I'm not going to paint the man as a complete monster. He wasn't violent – never laid a finger on either of us – and not unfaithful, as far as I'm aware. He was an excellent provider – and, in his own way, he *did* love us; but perhaps his idea of love was very different to mine.

It was always conditional, that was the trouble – you know, perhaps I'm taking it too literally, but to my mind, it can't be when you're married. It's supposed to be for better, for worse, but Alan only wanted the "better", could only be warm and kind when things went his way; and when it was "worse", the cold, condescending side came out. Take the whole thing with Dad – perhaps he'd have been more sympathetic, less dismissive, if it hadn't affected *him*. But, of course, he was worried about how I'd perform for that all-important dinner with Fred. *That* took preference over his wife's feelings, on such a difficult day – and okay, perhaps I *was* a bit dramatic, but it was my *dad*, for God's sake! I could never quite get past that – and yet, as with all these little incidents, I plodded on, convinced I'd somehow make it work.

In some ways, it might have been easier if he *had* hit me – easier to leave, I mean. When it's physical, you *know* it's wrong, there's no question – but when it's mental, it's so easy to convince yourself otherwise, because everyone argues, don't they? Imagine going to a refuge over a few cross words, when some of those women were afraid for their lives? I couldn't pretend it was the same – and yet I knew I was deeply unhappy, and my gut feeling was that something had to change. I didn't trust my gut then, though, and that's the thing with anxiety; you're never quite sure if it *is* your gut, or all in your stupid head...

As for the sex, even when I *really* hated it, it was never against my will, because I never said no. I'm not sure whether what *he* did changed – more likely my *perception* of it, because of what else was going on. All I'll say is that a few kind words make a world of difference. During the good times, I loved his dominance – he made me feel like a goddess, and I see now that *this* is what I wanted; *not* to feel stepped on or spoken to like crap! Whenever he was cold or critical, it seemed less like passion, more like control, and I couldn't handle that sudden change from officious to passionate – it was almost like two different people. But I never refused – because if I did, and he tried to force me.... I'm not saying he *would* have done – like I said before, he's *not* a monster – but I just didn't want to take that chance. I couldn't have ignored it, you see; and, just like if he'd hit me, I'd have had to get my head out of the sand.

And I couldn't do that – because if I admitted to myself that something wasn't right, I'd have had to admit that I shouldn't be with him; and where would that leave me and Dan?

There'd always be a home for us with Mum and Dad, but I didn't want to keep running to them *every* time anything was wrong. Besides, I was used to managing my own home and family now and going back would be hard – and it somehow felt like admitting defeat. So, if that was out of the equation, where else could I go? I had this real fear we'd end up somewhere awful.

And then, there was the whole question of Dan's education. He'd had enough disruption over the last few years – and I was just afraid that if we moved, he'd have to change schools like he did when we left Windle. You know, he's never admitted it to this day, but I'm still convinced he was bullied. So, imagine what might happen if we found ourselves on another council estate or, even worse, in some damp, grotty, inner-city flat? I know – I know – I sound like such a snob. After all, both Brian and I had come from working-class districts, there was no shame in it… But times had changed now, and so many places had gone downhill. I just wanted my boy to be safe – and I don't think many would blame me.

The friends he'd made since coming back to Liverpool were just like the ones he'd had in Windle. He was with them in Juniors for eighteen months or so, before they all moved together to high school; the same one Alan had gone to with his best friend, Bill Pegge. We'd been to church most Sundays on the lead-up; not because we really believed in it, but because the school was CofE.

It was known for top-notch results; the teachers took their time, and really seemed to care. Dan was doing brilliant, with A's in most subjects; only Maths was a bit more average, but not bad by any means – mainly B's, and certainly nothing below a C. He'd already decided he wanted to teach – probably English or Art. Of course, Maths was important, as he'd need his 'O' Level for teaching - but just passing it was enough. He didn't have to be exceptional. Anyway, 'O' Levels were a few years away – and when the time came, Alan would get him up to speed.

For all his faults, Alan was super-proud of Dan – always spoke of him in glowing terms to our friends; said he was a "good all-rounder" and had it in him to do anything he chose; and whatever that was, he'd give his utmost support. All Dan needed, he said, was that *tiny* bit of a push with the Maths – "but he'll get there in the end, darling – I've every faith in him.

Chapter Ten

And I suppose that's why I found it all so hard to take in – it knocked me for six, in all honesty. I knew Dan had become moody, and it was starting to worry me; this was why I had the chat with him in the first place. I'd expected those one-word answers I always got when he was keeping something in; so, I was quite surprised when he seemed ready to tell me – and completely shocked that it was so close to home.

In hindsight, of course, it makes complete sense. Alan drove *everyone* hard; me included, himself most of all – so, why *wouldn't* he have been that way with Dan? In our better times, he'd told me that he didn't do it to be cruel – he just believed in pushing people to their limits, as this was the only way for them to reach their full potential. *He'd* only got where he was by challenging himself to the hilt and not being satisfied with "half-baked half-measures". The all-or-nothing approach had worked for him, and he'd been told by his superiors that it made him a "first-rate" manager. Somehow, I'm not sure his underlings would have agreed… But with Dan, I don't know – I mean, he said he *loved* this boy, and you know, in spite of everything, I do think what he felt was real. I knew he was being a bit full-on over the Maths – but not like *that*….

I'd expected Dan to be a bit withdrawn for a while after his Grandad was poorly, but it seemed to be going on much longer than I'd thought – and to be getting that bit worse every day. It was starting to remind me of when we first moved to the estate, and so the first thing that entered my head was bullying…. But he seemed so happy at school and was always at his friends' houses…. Perhaps it was a teacher? He got on with most of them, although there was an elderly, grumpy chap that none of them could stand ("Waldorf", I think they called him). But, from all accounts, Waldorf was snappy with everyone; there was no particular problem with Dan, so it wasn't likely to be him.

The more I turned it over in my mind, the more I started with the "Wendy Worrifs", as Brian had jokingly called them. You heard so much about drugs, these days, and even younger kids being involved, and…what it, what if, what if…? And I knew I'd drive myself crazy until I asked him straight.

He was in his room, working on a project for his Art class. He and his mates had got really into Bowie, so the walls were covered in posters, and his painting was based on the cover of *"Ziggy Stardust"*.[ii] He'd turned 12 by this time; his shoulder-length hair now a light-mid-brown, in his bell-bottom jeans and red tank-top. It was a Saturday afternoon, and just me and him; Alan was off playing golf with Bill, and a couple of others from their schooldays. Decent, down-to-earth blokes – nothing like those stuffed-shirts he worked with.

Dan looked up briefly and smiled – he seemed deep in concentration. I sat on the edge of the bed.

"I know you're busy, son, but can we talk?"

He put down his brush, frowning slightly. "Okay…"

"Because I know you too well, and *something*'s on your mind."

"Yeah," he muttered "…yeah. You're right."

Straightaway, I was taken-aback – it was usually like getting blood out of a stone. "So, tell me, love – I'm sure it's nothing we can't sort out."

He paused for a moment, seeming to take a long, deep breath. "Alan said he'd send me to Borstal."

And I burst out laughing.

That's right – I laughed at my son. I won't make excuses; I'll just try and give you some idea of what was going on in my head.

I think most of us, in our age group, had that type of thing said to us as kids, growing up in those years just after the war. I'm not saying those times were as strict as when our parents were young, and certainly not our grandparents; but still, there were remnants of the old idea of "seen and not heard."

My mum and dad couldn't have been more loving, but Mum sometimes told us we'd "go in a home" if we didn't behave. To be fair, I think she only said it once to me – I can't remember what I'd done, but I must have back-chatted her in some way. But Jan was a pain in the backside, even then, a real little madam – always giving lip, constant tantrums…she had Mum at the end of her tether! Push and push, until she finally lost her rag. "Right, lady, that's enough! Any more of this, and I'll put you in a bloody *home*!" And no doubt Alan heard this too. I never knew his parents; his Mum died when he 14, his dad a few years before we met. I didn't know much about the mother, but I got the idea his dad could be quite harsh.

The problem is, though, each child is different – and that's why I made sure never to say anything like that to Dan, no matter what he'd done; even as a baby, I knew how sensitive he was... Once, when he was 3 or 4, he wouldn't get out of the bath. "Come on," I joked. "You'll end up going down the plughole, if you're not careful!" He was out like a shot – and the job I had, getting him back in!

Of course, we knew Mum didn't *mean* it. It was enough to make us take notice, mind, because we'd have to be edging *very* close to the line; but it didn't enter our heads that she'd actually *do* it! Even when she was furious, the love was always there. But I also think there's a difference between a *mother* chastising her kids, and a big, imposing man with a deep, powerful voice...I reckon that's why Dad never shouted, and always left that side of things to Mum – because he didn't want to scare us. We *respected* Mum, knew she'd take no messing, but we always felt safe...never afraid.

At this point, I had no clue of anything being wrong between Dan and Alan, or any altercation between them – whatever had gone on, it hadn't been in front of me. And I suppose I laughed because I knew Alan was bluffing, like Mum had with Jan, all those years ago. But at the same time, I guessed it would sound far more severe from someone like him than it would from my mum! And *Borstal*...what was *that* about?

So - I laughed, and no-one knows better than me that it wasn't my finest hour. But I stopped straightaway when I saw how hurt he looked, and I felt dreadful; still do.

"I'm so sorry, love," I said. "I know it's no joke. It's just – parents sometimes say things like that, but they wouldn't dream of going through with it. Like your nan, when me and Auntie Jan were kids. Tilly-mint, we called Jan - she had this way of pushing your nan's buttons – and I just thought back to those days – and it made me see the funny side."

"Nan's not like *him*," Dan muttered. "And he's *not* my parent. I've already got a dad."

"I know, son…I know…but look – I'm not defending what he said, here, but he wouldn't just say if from nowhere. There must have been some sort of argument?"

"Yeah," he admitted. "There was. And I told him to fuck off."

If I wasn't so sad, I might have laughed again – but only at how I imagined the look on Alan's face. Good for you, son, I thought – but, of course, I couldn't say that.

"Okay," I said. "So, I don't know what this disagreement between you was about, but it *was* cheeky of you, Dan, you must admit. You must have known he wouldn't be pleased - so why would you say something like that?"

"Because he just kept going on and wouldn't shut up. It was when Grandad wasn't well. I could see you were upset, because he said what's the problem, Grandad's fine now…. You told me to go up and do my homework… and I could hear him still on about it when you were washing up. Then the next thing, he came in here, and started saying it to me. And all this stuff about needing to man up, and stop being a wuss…So, I tried telling him, I'm *not* a wuss - this is my *Grandad* - but he wouldn't listen – didn't get it…. And I was getting more and more angry inside – then it just came out."

What could I say to that? I'd felt exactly the same.

"I thought he was gonna hit me," he went on, "but he said it's not his style. His dad would've done it to *him*, but *he*'s not like that. But if I didn't watch out, he'd send me away to a school for horrible kids. He said they used to be called "approved schools", or something like that, but the name had changed now – he wasn't sure what to."

My head was spinning by now. I was fuming with Alan, but at the same time, knew he'd never *do* it in a million years….

"Look, love," I said, "it was an awful thing for him to say, and I can see how much it's affected you. And you're right about how he was over Grandad – I don't blame you for being angry. But what he said about that school – I honestly think it was in the heat of the moment – to shock you, because of the swearing."

He shook his head. "No, Mum. He said it was part of it, but there was more to it than that – and this thing about a camel…"

"The straw that broke the camel's back?"

"Yeah – that's it – and when I swore, that's what I'd done. He hadn't been happy with me for a while, he said, and he's disappointed with my attitude – that I'm lazy, and take things for granted, and that's why I only get B's for Maths – and he knows I can do better. And if I don't buck my ideas up, he'll think about sending me to one of these places. And since then, if I don't get an A, he gives me this *look*. Then, when you're not around, he says it's not good enough – and remember what we talked about. But I've tried and tried for the A's, Mum – I just can't seem to do it.

"I was dreading my school report, because I knew I'd only get a B …. I was having nightmares about those places - and then, I don't know why, but one day I thought, maybe I should find out more about them – perhaps they're not as bad as they sound. So, I asked the Duke if he'd heard of approved schools, and did he know what they were like? I didn't mention Alan, though – just said I'd seen something about them on telly…."

"The Duke" was their nickname for an English teacher everyone loved – Mr. Ellingham. I can only guess they called him that because of Duke Ellington, although that did surprise me a bit. Somehow, I can't see jazz appealing to kids, but who knows – I could be wrong.

"So, the Duke said yeah- he did know about them – but they weren't really schools, more like prisons. 'You've heard of Borstal?' he asked me. 'Well, approved school's what they used to call them' And then he said it was like when an adult went to jail – the same sort of place, but for kids who'd done really bad things – and gone to court and been found guilty.

"I felt relieved then – because I'd have to have done something awful, and only a *judge* could send me there – not *him*! He'd just said it to make me try harder – but I was worried sick, Mum! I even threw up some nights, when I knew he'd be looking at my homework… But it was all a lie – and that's why I hate him."

Since then, I've realized that the Duke might have been slightly wrong – and although those approved schools were *similar* to Borstal, they weren't one and the same. I believe there *was* a new name for them, but it was something like "community homes". I don't think it was exactly "prison", like Borstal was – but that's not the point. There's no doubt that both were tough, tough places; and my husband had used them to threaten my boy, dangling them over him every time he didn't perform to *his* standards. And make no mistake, he wanted Dan to get all A's for *himself* – so he could boast about his "gifted" stepson, and how *he*'d found the best in him. No doubt he did this sort of thing to his staff – I could just picture them, terrified of getting the push for the slightest mistake; and guessed they must hate him, too.

But what could I do…what the hell could I do? Because what was the alternative, when leaving would be even worse? Of course, I see *now* that this wasn't the case, but back then…well, as I said, I just couldn't get past the thought of us ending up in a slum, and Dan getting beaten senseless by thugs in an inner-city school. The bullying there would be *far* worse than anything

Alan could do, and - what if, what if, what if? But at the same time, how could I stay with a man who did that to my son? Perhaps he *hadn't* meant to go that far, or thought Dan wouldn't take him seriously – but the fact remained, he'd had him scared witless, convinced he'd end up in some boot-camp, for nothing at all. I couldn't forgive that – but what could I do…what could I do?

And as I felt the panic, I did the very thing that drove his dad away. I blamed it all on Dan.

Chapter Eleven

Sometimes, in my darker days, I'd wonder if being with Alan was some sort of come-uppance, for how I'd treated Brian. Perhaps we were two of a kind; and I deserved a bully, because *I* was a bully....

Brian's never taken life too seriously, and that was at the heart of it. And by that, I don't mean selfish, like Jan, or irresponsible – just that he has this "worse things happen at sea" attitude when anything goes wrong. He's right, of course - and when I think of how worked-up I used to get, it was never because anyone had died, or taken ill, or anything remotely near it. Just things like the supermarket running out of our usual cereal, or someone being five minutes late.

The thing about lateness was the worst. I can't bear to be late for anything – I suppose it's how I was brought up, but it just seems a bit rude. But as for Brian, well – this is nothing against his family, they're kind, good people – but a bit come-day, go-day. "You know me, love," his mother says, "you take me as you find me." She always has friends and neighbours popping in, uninvited. It's a lovely, relaxed atmosphere - but too chaotic for me. And I'm not saying my family are "posh" in any way – Mum's from Everton, Dad from Anfield, both solidly working-class – but somehow, they just seem that bit more "proper". They watch their manners, like everything in its place – always turn up on time, and certainly not unannounced!

Brian, on the other hand, never seemed in the least bit bothered about being late, and that drove me insane. I can remember ruining our anniversary – 4th or 5th, it must have been – because of a stupid row over a taxi. Dan was with his nan and grandad for the evening, and Brian and I had booked a pub meal – the Bird i' th' Hand in Thatto Heath, I think, which wasn't far, but not close enough to walk. We'd decided on the cab so Bri could have a drink, and had it ordered for 7.15, to get there at half-past.

It got to 7.20; there was still no sign of the taxi, and I got myself in a state.

"It's alright," Bri said, "I'll call them, and find out what's the hold-up."

"Just tell them to hurry, Bri – the restaurant won't be pleased."

"Okay- but it's not school, you know, Wend," he laughed. "You won't get detention!"

And that was what made me see red.

"Trust you to make a bloody joke of it!" I snapped. "And *you* don't know what they'll be like – they might give our table to someone else."

"I doubt it, love – they won't be busy on a Tuesday. In fact, we probably didn't need to book at all."

"Yeah, but you *would* say that, Brian," I shot back. "That's you all over! Never want to plan, or get yourself organized…"

He sighed. "Not this again."

"Yes, *this* again! Because *I* wanted to order it for 7, just in case it was delayed, but *no*…. quarter-past's fine, you said!"

"So, it's my fault - as usual?"

"Well, I could have told you this would happen, Bri, but you just think I'm fussing over nothing…"

"Here we are," he said, as we heard the cab pull up. "No harm done, eh?"

And with that, I stormed out to tell the driver to forget it. We didn't need him anymore; we'd waited too long.

So, I guess that gives you an idea of what I meant, when I said I'd have left me, too….

In fairness to myself, I wasn't *always* like this. It's just when you're struggling, constantly, to keep the nerves at bay, and it's a real balancing act – and you feel you might *just* be getting there, then something throws you off kilter. It might be small, or insignificant, but that one thing is all it takes. I know Brian was just trying to keep it light and help me see the funny side, but while I usually loved his sense of humour, it didn't work when I was "on one"; and it soon became too easy to take things out on him.

Our last row was two months before he left. He'd gone out after work for someone's 30th – bear in mind, he didn't often do this – and I got worked up about the time he'd be home. He wasn't close friends with this person, so he wouldn't be staying long – just a couple of pints, and back around 9ish, he said.

Well, it got to 9.15, and I started imagining him in an accident. He hadn't taken the car that night, so would be back on the bus – perhaps he'd had had too much to drink, not looked where he was going, and been knocked down…

9.20. Maybe it *wasn't* an accident. You hear of one thing leading to another at these office parties – he might have got off with a girl from work…

9.30. A knock on the door. No – it's not a girl; it *is* an accident, and this is the police…I open the door, fully expecting to see two of them, a man and a woman (they always send a woman to break bad news); and there's Brian, standing there grinning. "Sorry, love – forgot me key."

I flew at him. He tried to explain that he'd just missed a bus, and there was no phone box nearby to call me, but I didn't want to know; just kept shouting that it was *typical* of him – he was thoughtless, inconsiderate- and I was sorry I married him.

I've no idea why I said that – but, when I'm at my worst, this is what happens. These things just seem to fly out of my mouth, and I *know* I don't mean it – and yet, part of me *does*, because I'm angry, and upset, and I want *them* to understand how I feel…. And somehow, by doing it, it gives me the sense of release I'm looking for – while at the same time, totally despising myself.

Brian seemed to recoil, and there was this look in his eyes – not just hurt – it's hard to describe, but I knew straightaway there'd be no getting through this.

"Bri," I said, "I didn't mean…."

"It's okay," he said flatly. "You're upset. Don't worry. It's okay."

But we both knew it wasn't – and that's why there was no shock when he went.

Chapter Twelve

And that afternoon, when Dan told me what had gone on with Alan, the panic was exactly the same. Thinking back to the night when Brian was late, I'd felt just as trapped and helpless as I did now. The situations were totally different; but in both, it seemed that nothing *I* could do could change it. And just in that split second, I felt furious with Dan, as I'd been so often with his dad.

Why did he have to wind Alan up? If he hadn't done that, the rest of it wouldn't have followed on – and I wouldn't be in this dilemma. And I'd been *managing* – making the best of it….!

So, the next thing, I'm launching into this tirade. I can't remember exactly what I said – just that I was screaming at him, telling him how ungrateful he was; that he was *lucky* to have such a nice home, and a step-dad who actually cared about him, and showed an interest… and it was his *own* fault that Alan had said what he did – his own, stupid fault, for swearing at him… and we *all* got things said to us sometimes, that we didn't like – but that's just the way life is, and he had to get on with it, and grow up….

And all the while, I can see Dan recoil – and that look in his eyes, where I knew there'd be no going back. Almost an exact re-run of that last row with Brian; but far worse, because this was my boy.

"You asked me, Mum," he said at last. "I only told you because you asked."

The thing that broke my heart the most was that he looked *resigned*. Sad, but not shocked – like he'd expected this reaction, but had taken the chance, in the hope, however small, of being wrong.

I swallowed hard. "Look," I managed, "I'm so sorry I shouted, Danny – it's just difficult… you know…"

"It's okay."

"Are you sure?"

"Yeah."

"And… look, you will still come to me, love, won't you – if something's wrong?"

"Yeah."

"You won't be afraid to tell me?"

"No."

"Okay – good. So, we'll try and move on now – say no more about it?"

He took another deep breath. "Yeah."

He came down an hour or so later; all seemed back to normal, and it wasn't mentioned again, as we agreed. I knew deep-down that he *wasn't* okay – but perhaps, somehow, I could fix it. If I could *just* work on Alan, and get him to see that Maths wasn't the be-all-and-end-all... It was a long-shot; but if I *did* persuade him to ease off, they might start getting on again – and Dan would see I *was* on his side, after all.

Alan must have won at the golf – he got home in a good mood that night, and it lasted the next few days. You never know, I thought; you never know....

Chapter Thirteen

I'd just about managed to convince myself that it could work. I made the most of Alan's good mood, doing all I could to keep him sweet. Pathetic, I know, and I hated myself for it; but I had to remind myself that this was for my boy's sake....

But then he belittled me again – and this time, it wasn't just me who noticed.

If there's one thing I *didn't* regret about meeting Alan, it's that it led me to Barb and Bill. To be honest, that was another thing that scared me about leaving; I'd grown so close to Barb over the last few years, but if I split up with Alan, that was bound to end. The three of them went back a long time – way before Alan met me – and he'd known Bill for most of his life.

Bill was best man at our wedding; that was the first time I'd met him and, I must admit, I wasn't too sure what to make of him. I knew he and Alan had grown up together, and that their fathers were also best friends; and that Bill's dad Arthur had been a stonemason, like Alan's dad John. Bill had followed him into the trade but had a few extra strings to his bow – he'd also trained in plumbing and joinery, and had done all three over the years. These days he ran a carpentry business; it was really successful, so it went without saying that, like Alan, he'd be driven, determined and extremely capable.

He certainly was all this, but the similarity ended there, and I think this was what surprised me; because the one thing I hadn't expected was for Bill to be *quiet*. Not shy – when he *did* have something to say, it was always with confidence, sureness and authority; in fact, he was one of the few people that Alan ever took notice of. But he didn't speak often, or for the sake of it, preferring to listen and observe. I noticed he always seem to get along with Dan, and guessed this was because Dan, too, was a people-watcher.

The other difference was that Bill was modest – didn't need to go on about how brilliant he was, and let his actions speak for themselves. He also seemed willing to learn from others; keep an open mind, I remember he once said. No-one knows *everything*; there's always *something* you won't have thought of, and it's good to have that fresh pair of eyes. Now, I know I've got no clue about running my own business – but, to my mind, that made perfect sense.

Perhaps because he did such a physical job, Bill was rugged and intensely masculine – almost off the scale! But I also think he'd be that way whatever work he did – it was just *in* him, and that might have been why Alan was slightly in awe. Alan's version of manly was much more "polished" - and, again, just *different*.

Bill walked with purpose, but never strutted or preened – wouldn't have felt the need to. His voice was low, almost gruff. He was very tall and very burly; a receding hairline, even in his 30s, and a "lumberjack"-style beard. He dressed a bit like a lumberjack too (although not at the wedding, obviously!), always in jeans and plaid-check flannel shirts. But underlying all this was a gentleness, almost a softness. I sometimes wondered how

he balanced the two, but when I think about it, I should have
seen it's not that hard – my dad always managed it fine…
Although Bill generally looked quite serious, he'd sometimes
break out into a mischievous smile and wry humour. You could
see the warmth in him, and how much he adored Barb – she's a
lucky woman, I thought. He was besotted – but then, who
wouldn't have been?

Still, I was a little wary of Bill at first, and it took a while to
warm up. That wasn't because I didn't like him – I just wasn't
sure what he thought of me! I always do that when someone's
quiet, and I know I'm wrong. It was the same when Dan had
that girlfriend, Lori; she must have picked up on it, and I'm
sorry for that. Still not convinced she was the one for *him*, but
that's by-the-by....

But if I had any doubts about Bill, they were all cleared up that
time he gave me a hand with the washing-up. It was usually me
and Barb in the kitchen, while the blokes watched the footie. I
know… but it gave us a chance for a really good catch-up, and I
always enjoyed that. And I suppose that's why it surprised me
when Bill helped; because it was always Barb, I just assumed that
Bill, like Alan, did nothing at home.

In saying that, I suppose I'm a bit unfair. It wasn't that Alan did
nothing – just that he believed so strongly that there were men's
jobs and women's jobs, and that these could never, ever cross
over; and that *his* jobs were strictly outdoors. Apart from
decorating, of course, which he always did brilliantly – I'll give
him that. He looked after the garden and the car, and any

maintenance on the house, and don't get me wrong, I'm grateful for that. These days, now I've got my flat, I'm quite glad that the landlord takes care of those things – I'm hopeless at DIY, and it's not Dan's forte, either; he might be fantastic with a paint-brush, but not *that* kind...

So, all things considered, I suppose it might seem a fair exchange; after all, he *did* work hard, and I *was* home all day. It was just, I honestly don't think he knew how much went into running that place. And perhaps, because he'd never been involved in it, he'd assumed it was easy; he'd always got professional cleaners in before we married (his first wife hadn't been there long), and had sent his laundry out. Of course, I knew those things were for working people short on time, and I'm not for one minute saying I expected to *keep* them; but at the same time, I wasn't sat there doing nothing, and just *some* understanding of that would have been nice....

The house had four bedrooms and two bathrooms, one on each floor – an enormous kitchen, and in the front room was this ornate fireplace that was a bugger to keep clean. That might have been fine if I could have focused on one room, or maybe a couple of rooms a day, or took one day a week to completely blitz it. But it ended up being the whole thing, from top-to-bottom, *every single day*! Because if it was anything less than perfect, there'd be comments. He'd notice the slightest thing out of place, the smallest speck of dust. "Falling down on the job, eh?" Or that *look* – the one he gave me that day when Dad was ill. And I'd feel, not just small, or inadequate, but – almost like an *employee*. As though I was being appraised or evaluated – and he did this by searching for the tiniest mistake.

It took hours to clean – especially that damned fireplace – and then there was that particular way he liked his clothes ironed, and those elaborate meals he expected (I didn't dare do sausage and mash again!). I'd be exhausted by the evening, and even then, there wasn't an end to it; he'd have me up and down for the rest of the night, keeping him topped up with drinks. No doubt fair in his eyes – after all, I'd had *all day* to relax...!! Again, if it wasn't "just-so", or done as quickly as he'd like, it would be picked up on. That "must try harder" look – like poor Dan with those bloody Maths....

.... So, anyway, there was this one evening when Barb and Bill were due round, but only Bill turned up with their daughter, Emily. Barb suffered quite badly with migraines, and they'd often come on all at once. It had happened that night; but rather than let us down, she'd told them both to go ahead without her. I did feel a little disappointed, but then chided myself straightaway – poor Barb was ill, and I should be thinking of her, not *me*! But it wasn't meant selfishly – I just loved her company.

Em was a lovely, level-headed girl – flame-haired, like her mum, and tall, like her dad. She was slightly older than Dan; they got on great, and at one point, later down the line, I wondered if they'd get together. It never happened, but they were always close. So, they were chatting about music (Em loved Bowie too), while Alan and Bill talked (well, Bill *listened*) about cricket, golf, but mainly work. And that left me, myself and I, like a fifth wheel, out of the conversation and clearing up after everyone.

As I put the dishes in soak, a little forlornly, I heard Alan calling through - "We're still waiting for our coffee, you know, darling! Don't fall down on the job, now, will you?" Then he laughed. "Honestly, Bill! Women, eh?"

I felt myself choking up, which was nothing new. "Coffee," I told myself, firmly. "Come *on – coffee*! Get a grip!"

Like everything else, Alan liked his coffee a certain way - wouldn't entertain "that instant rubbish". It would take a few minutes to grind the beans, then more time to percolate, so I'd have to get to it; otherwise, he'd be calling me again, and it was embarrassing with people here.... But then the dishes were there, piled up, and he'd have something to say about that, too.... I'd have to get the coffee to them, then come straight back in here to finish off, in the hope he wouldn't ask what I was doing, and why it was taking so long? I started feeling flustered, and annoyed at myself – why was I always so bloody *slow*?

Next thing, "I'll give you a hand, love." - and there's Bill at the sink. "I'll get these put away – and you can sort the coffee for Soft-Lad." He winked, and there was that sudden, cheeky grin.

"No, honestly, Bill, it's fine..." I began. (No doubt there'd be comments later...).

"No probs," he said, in that plain-speaking, gruff-but-kind way of his. "Least I can do. I'd have offered before, to be honest, but I know you and Barb like your chats…"

He was ploughing through the dishes, and already had half of them put away.

"You're a dab hand," I remarked. "Barb's got you well-trained!"

"Well - gotta do your bit, haven't you?"

"Who knows?" I smiled. "Perhaps you could teach his nibs?"

"Oh, aye," he laughed. "Just before Hell freezes over?"

And for the first time, I wondered if this friendship might be one-sided – and not on Bill's side...

As expected, it was pointed out later how decent of Bill it was to help, when I was falling behind; but somehow, I didn't feel quite as shit as usual. That was a good while before we separated – maybe eighteen months or so into the marriage – but from then on, I knew Bill was my friend too.

As for Barb – well, what can I say?

Beautiful, inside and out – that sounds like a bit of a cliché, doesn't it? But with Barb, it was all true, and the only *real* way you could describe her. Warm, funny, clever; inspirational.

On the face of it, Barb was Bill's complete, polar opposite. Tiny (just under five feet), bubbly, a huge extrovert and a real "girlie-girl". She'd been a hairdresser before Em was born, and had her own hair in a variety of colours and styles; when I first met her, it was "disco curls" in a rich, vibrant red. Her style was sexy and sassy; she loved make-up, false nails and lashes, jewellery (especially earrings) and dressing up, even to go shopping!

They'd met at 18; Bill was still doing his plumbing apprenticeship and was fixing a broken pipe at the salon where she worked in Garston. By all accounts, many had seen this lively, fun-loving girl and her reserved, rather intense young man as an unlikely couple. She loved going out dancing; he preferred a quiet pint - and "spit and sawdust", real-ale pubs at that! And while she loved soul and disco, he liked country rock – the Eagles, Lynard Skynard, Dr. Hook. But they weren't so different at heart – not when it came to the important stuff; they both had the same compassion, stood up for the underdog – and couldn't abide any form of bullying.

For all her seeming frivolity, there was nothing shallow about Barb. She was far more intelligent than some gave her credit for; including Alan, who seemed to regard her with an amused tolerance. I could tell straight-off that she was well aware of this; there was often banter between them, and although friendly in tone, I could tell that underneath, she was mocking his pompous ways for real.

Barb had an enquiring mind – questioned everything, and read voraciously – fact and fiction, old and new; from the heavyweight classics to throw-away trash for the beach. Whenever she spoke of these books, she brought them to life in such a vivid way, with *her* brand of warmth and humour; even if you hated reading, you couldn't fail to be drawn in.Her mother had once told her she should be a teacher; and once Em had started high school, that's what she did.

Her original plan had been to return to hairdressing, which she'd never really wanted to give up. She'd always loved it, and the girls she worked with in the salon – and when her mum, Bridie, offered to look after Em when she was born, it seemed the perfect solution. But her plans would sadly change when Bridie died of a brain tumour, aged just 43, when Em was two months old. Barb never got over that completely; but she turned it round, and it was in memory of her mum that when she did return to work, it was teaching she decided on. When I met her, she'd just started her training, and in no doubt she'd made the right choice; she was born for it.

Bridie, from the sound of her, was also a clever woman, much under-estimated. She'd been regularly top of her class at school but, unlike my mum's neighbour, Mrs. O'Rourke, had no chance to take this further; she left school at 14 to start factory work, which she did until her marriage to husband Hugh, in 1942.Both Bridie and Hugh had grown up poor, in tenements near Toxteth Dock, and had got a house in Speke in 1944 – not long before Barb was born. Hugh worked on the docks, while Bridie stayed at home, except occasional cleaning jobs when they were short. But she read whenever she could get the time – and often told Barb that if things had been different, the one thing she'd have loved to do was teach.

The further Barb got with her studies, the more deeply she got into feminism – although it was *always* in her, she said. She'd questioned patriarchy from a young age, strongly feeling the injustice that her mother's class and gender gave her so little choice. Of course, she knew that she was as un-typical a feminist as you could possibly get, but that was fine, she said – it was all about what you did, not what you looked like.

In the early days, I wondered what Bill made of it all. He was such a man's man – no new-age hippie – and I guessed that he, like Alan, would favour traditional roles. It went without saying that Alan thought it was rubbish, "a nonsense", he called it, and I think I made that same mistake of assuming Bill would be the same. In fact, he was nothing but supportive of Barb; "did his bit" around the house, as he called it (it was probably more than a bit, to be fair); showed an interest in her work, and just seemed so genuinely *proud* of what she was achieving. And yes, they had their ups and downs, like everyone, but it was heart-warming to see how they were with each other; I loved them too much to even think of being jealous!

Chapter Fourteen

Alan's good mood continued for a couple more weeks, and I began to think my "keep him sweet" plan was working. On the Saturday (a fortnight after I'd screamed at Dan), we were due to have Bill and Barb over for a meal, just the four of us; Em had a sleep-over at her friend's, and it was Dan's monthly trip to see his dad.

Dan always went to Brian's on the Friday - the only one in the month not spent at his nan's. They had their usual routine, with Sue picking him up, and Brian bringing him home on the Sunday evening; only ever dropped him off, though. Never came in – just sat for a moment, watching to see Dan safely inside, before he drove away. He'd only met Alan once, but it was probably enough to suss out he wouldn't be made welcome….

But this time, for some reason, it was Brian who turned up on the Friday evening, quite a bit later than we'd expected Sue. Dan thought a lot of Sue, and I could see him getting anxious (as I was) in case she'd had an accident – although I guess that wasn't the only thing on his mind…

Sue worked in the same department as Brian, in a similar role, but only part-time – Monday to Wednesday, I think; but this Friday she was tied up because Abby (her daughter from her first marriage) was ill, and she couldn't leave her. Anyway, Bri had managed to sort out an early finish, so he'd be able to come for Dan. The doorbell went just before 6, and I was taken aback, and just a little annoyed, to see him stood there, with that daft grin on his face – just like the time he forgot his key.

"Sorry I'm late," he said, and explained about Abby being poorly; and of course, I knew it couldn't be helped. Still, I thought, typical Brian, not calling to give me the heads-up….

But, at the same time, it was good to see him. At least he was kind – always kind, not just when the mood took… He hadn't changed much; hair a bit shorter, maybe – but still the same old, laid-back Bri.

"Hope Abby gets well soon," I said. "Oh, and long time, no see, by the way!"

"Yeah," he smiled, "Been a while, eh, love? How's tricks?"

"Oh, not bad, you know – can't grumble. You?"

"Same here – just plodding on, really – as always."

"Dan, love!" I called. "Your dad's here!"

It was clearly a surprise for Dan too – a good one, judging from the joy on his face at seeing him. And I suddenly felt tearful, as I thought how glad he must be to get away. Brian must have picked up on it.

"You get yourself settled in the car, son," he said to Dan, "I'll be there in a sec."

"Bye, love," I said.

"See you, Mum." All fine on the surface, but just that *something* not quite the same. Perhaps he'd tell Brian and Sue, this weekend – about how shit I'd been…

"You okay, Wend?" Bri asked. "You look a bit upset."

"You know me." I tried to laugh. "Never could hold my water! I'll just miss him, that's all – but I'll be fine."

"He'll be back before you know it."

"I know… as I say, it's just me being daft."

He looked at me for a moment – quite serious, for him, and even slightly frowning. "Listen, love, are you *sure* you're alright? You seem a bit on edge."

"Yeah!" I said lightly. "Yeah! Never better! Just been a busy week, and – you know – *that* time of month."

"Oh, right - I did wonder if it was that, but I didn't wanna say – it might sound like I'm being a chauvinist."

"No, it doesn't, hon. And you're not – you're definitely not!"

"That's good to know!" He laughed. "You'll have to remind Sue of that, next time I leave the bog-seat up! Bloody men, she says…" We both smiled. "All in jest, of course. So, anyway - how's your hubby?"

"Not too bad," I said evenly. "Flat out at work. He's regional manager now, and…"

I tailed off as the car pulled up in the drive. I could see from Alan's face that he wasn't one bit pleased to see Brian. He was also stressed to hell – even more than usual; he almost fell getting out of the car, only just managing to stop himself, but in doing this he dropped his briefcase. It flew open; the papers scattered.

"*Shit!*"

He'd recently started wearing glasses – only for driving, but he still had them on. They fell off as he bent to gather the papers.

"Shit!" he said again. "Jesus bloody *Christ!*"

Then Brian smirked. "Enjoy your trip, lad?"

(Trust you, Bri! I thought – although I must admit, I nearly laughed myself).

Alan didn't reply – just glowered at him, before retrieving his specs and snapping shut the case. Noticing Dan in Brian's car, he tried to catch his attention, but Dan was looking the other way; perhaps deliberately.

"Sorry about that, fella," Bri said to Alan. "Just messing around – Wend knows what I'm like."

"Indeed," Alan muttered, looking him up and down, superciliously; just like when they met the first time.

"Well, anyway," Brian continued, uneasily, "have a good evening, mate."

Alan nodded curtly, before storming off into the house. Brian shrugged. "Blimey – *someone*'s had a bad day!"

"I know – it's like I said, work's mad busy for him right now."

"Nightmare, eh? Hope it calms down – no job's worth the hassle! Anyway – nice to see you, kidda." Then I noticed that worried, almost-frown had returned. "And listen, you look after yourself – okay?"

I nodded. "You too, hon. Speak soon."

I braced myself for the comments about Brian. Shame he missed Dan, was all he said, but I kept an open mind. It wouldn't be *that* easy. He hardly spoke during dinner, and I knew what was brewing; especially when he started pushing the food around his plate, squashing the veg down with the fork. They were cooked slightly more than usual – only by a fraction – but had turned to mush by the time he'd finished with them.

"Inedible, I'm afraid," he remarked, at last.

Look, he *is* my son's dad, I nearly said - but no… let it blow over…

He spent most of the next day in his study – accounts he needed to look over, he said, and hadn't had a minute in the office. All good, I thought – with any luck, he'll work off his bad mood… But when he finally emerged that evening, just as Barb and Bill arrived, he still looked tense, and I could always tell when he was in that fault-finding frame of mind. Not just from his face, or voice, or even body-language; hard to explain, but just *something*, and I always knew how it would end up. And tonight, it wasn't just aimed at me. As I got the meals dished up, I could overhear him picking an argument with Barb.

"I saw your lot on the box last night."

"*My* lot?" Barb asked. "What d'you mean, Al?"

"You know – the Women's Rights Brigade!" He laughed. "The '*Sisterhood*', if you will! Quite enlightening. They kept banging on about men being so terrible - and I wondered what *you* think, Bill? Perhaps you should remember all this, next time a tyre needs changing…"

"Leave it, Al," Bill said sternly, as I brought the plates through. "We came for a meal, not a row."

"Oh, come *on*, Bill!" He laughed again. "It's not a *row* – just a healthy debate – isn't that right, Barb?"

They *did* sometimes have these little spats, but it was usually good-natured - and tonight, as I say, there was definitely an edge. Barb could obviously sense this; she usually gave as good as she got (or often better), but this time she wisely didn't rise to it.

As I sat down, I felt, for a moment, furious with Brian – for turning up without warning yesterday, and making one of his stupid jokes, and – *trust him*! But, no, I thought, that's unfair; it's not *always* Brian's fault - I can't keep doing that… And besides anything, whatever Alan felt about Brian, it had *nothing* to do with Bill and Barb! We ate in awkward silence; I'd made beef bourguignon, and I was just *waiting* for something to be wrong with it… But no – it seemed to go down well…

"Hmm…not bad at all," he nodded, finishing his plate. "Bit lighter on the seasoning, next time, maybe – but a really good effort. More than makes up for that disaster with the veg last night! But still – we all make mistakes."

I could just imagine him saying it to Dan – along with "better next time, eh?", "you'll get there in the end", and all the other "encouraging" remarks that made you feel like crap… Well done for getting seven A's, son – shame about that B to drag you down, but never mind – *we all make mistakes…*

"Jesus Christ, Al!" I heard Bill mutter under his breath.

Then I felt Barb's arm around my shoulder. "It's okay, hon," she said, as I found myself in tears.

To be completely fair, Alan did soften when he saw this – and I think it shocked him.

"Look, my darling – I don't know what's brought all this on, but I was telling you how *well* you'd done. It was meant as a *compliment.*"

"Yeah," Barb said furiously, "a bloody back-handed one!"

Then she tore into him. Told him she couldn't stand him – never *had* been able to stand him! And that he was a gobshite, and a sexist pig, and nothing but a bully; and she didn't know how I put up with him – or how *Bill* put up with him, for that matter…!

"Are you quite finished?" he asked – his expression the same, I guessed, as when Dan told him where to get off.

Barb shook her head. "Not even *started*, lad! I mean, *look* at her! She's in *bits*, here, and that's all down to you, Al – the one who's meant to *love* her, for fuck's sake! And Wendy's a lovely person – a *gorgeous* person – and *you* – you're lucky to have her!"

"Do you think I don't know that?" His voice cracked – and I remembered why I'd never thought of leaving.

The money, the security – it played a big part; no point in pretending it didn't. But there *was* more to it, and it was this – because *sometimes*, I'd get a glimpse of who he was; or at least of who he *might* have been, if all the bluff and bravado was peeled away....

"Look," he said to Bill. "You and I go back a long time, and *you* know I'm not – well, not like..." He tailed off – and I think we all knew he was talking about his father. "I know my faults, Bill," he continued. "I've been told I'm blunt, sometimes to the point of rudeness – and opinionated – and like a dog with a bone if I think I'm right. All true – and, you know, in my line of work, it's not always a bad thing! But one thing I am *not* is a bully! I won't accept that, Bill – and you *know* it's not true – we've been friends for years."

Bill sighed. "No, Al – I've *tolerated* you for years."

"Oh!" Again, there was that slight crack; and despite it all, I did feel for him. I knew what Bill meant to him, and that couldn't have been easy to hear. But then he cleared his throat. "Oh –

well. No use beating around the bush, I suppose. Thanks for your feedback."

"You see, this is what I mean," Bill went on. "You don't even speak like a normal person, anymore! It's like we're in that bloody office of yours, instead of just mates getting together … You were alright when we were kids, but now…. I hate to say it, Al, but since getting that job, you've turned into one jumped-up prick! And Barb's right - you order Wendy about, like she's some bloody skivvy, and it's all wrong - all wrong."

"Okay," Alan nodded, matter-of-factly. "Okay. Well, as I said – best to be upfront, isn't it? Because it seems a bit ridiculous, keeping up the charade – dinner parties, and whatnot – a waste of everyone's time and effort, really. So, okay. Let's call it a night, shall we?"

"Come on, love," Bill muttered to Barb. "Let's get out of here."

"I'll get your coats," I sobbed. "And I'm so sorry – this is all my fault – things are okay, really…" That desperate part of me, still clinging on. "I'm just missing Dan, and everything gets to me more. But I didn't mean for this…"

"It's not your fault, lovely," Barb said, hugging me. "Don't you even think of blaming yourself. And listen – if you need to get away for a bit, you can always come back with us, you know – for a night, or as long as you want."

"No… thanks, Barb, but no…it's fine… honestly."

"Alright." Barb sighed. "But the offer's always there."

"Yeah," Bill added. "You know where we are, love."

Alan didn't move from the dining table.

"I'm going up," I muttered. "My head's banging." No doubt he'd have some remark about the dishes being left – but I was past caring. "Goodnight, then."

"You see, this is what happens," he said. "I've told you so often, Wendy, about controlling your emotions – but you *can't* seem to do it. And now…" He sighed. "My whole life, I've known that man …But perhaps there's a lesson to be learnt, here."

"You know what?" I heard myself say. "I think I *will* go to Barb's, after all."

Chapter Fifteen

"I'm leaving *home*," Dan said, determinedly. He was two years old, and not best pleased that Mummy had stopped him playing in the sandpit ("My New Brighton", he called it); but it *was* past his bedtime after all…

"That's fine," I said. We were all there, laughing – me and Bri, Mum, Dad and Jan. "Shall I pack your bag?"

"No!" he shouted. "Don't *want* that one!"

"Oh, aye," Brian smiled. "Travelling light, eh? Brave lad!"

"I'm going," Dan insisted. "Bye-bye!"

"Bye-bye!" we all waved, as he toddled off towards the front door. He turned round, to see us all still waving – and again, now not so sure. "I go tomorrow…"

"I think that's a good idea," I said.

…. Years later, I'd remember that day when he went for real – hoping and praying that somehow, it would end the same. That he'd get as far as the bus stop, then turn back – I won't go today, Mum – maybe tomorrow – maybe never.

But I was thinking of it that night, too – the night I left Alan; because I knew he didn't believe, for one minute, that I'd actually *do* it.

"I'll bring your case down," he said, as I finished off my packing. Humouring me, like I'd done with Dan. "And I've only had a glass of wine – I can drive you, if you like."

"No need," I said flatly. "I've got money left over from the shopping. I'll get a cab."

"It's no trouble."

"I know, but as I said, Alan – I'd rather not. Anyway, there's still Dan's case to do yet."

He followed me through to Dan's room – sat on the edge of the bed.

"Will Bill and Barb have space for you both?" he asked. "Because as far as I'm aware, they only have one spare room."

I shrugged. "If not, I'm sure he'll be fine to stay with Mum and Dad for a bit – just till I've sorted myself out. He loves spending time with them, as you know."

"Fair enough."

He watched in silence as I folded Dan's clothes. Once they were in the case, I started to take down the posters – he'd no doubt want to keep them.

"For God's sake, Wendy," Alan said at last. "Don't tell me you're thinking of going *through* with this nonsense?"

"Yes," I said. "And the fact you call it 'nonsense' makes me all the more certain."

He shook his head. "I don't know... I don't know. I'm at a loss, really. I mean, you want for nothing. And if you say that's not important, I'll beg to differ - I *know* how unhappy you were on that bloody council estate. And I've never cheated – wouldn't dream of raising a hand to you."

"You make it sound like you're doing me some sort of favour – but guess what, Alan? You're not *supposed* to!"

"I'm not a bad man, Wendy – that's all I'm saying." He sighed heavily – and I think he was beginning to see I meant business. "Alright – so, what is it, exactly, that I'm supposed to have done?"

"You belittle me," I said. "It's all the time. Every little thing that doesn't *quite* reach your standards – and even when it does, you just *have* to remind me of when it didn't. Like before – you couldn't resist letting everyone know I'd messed up yesterday – only this time, it backfired, because they took my side. And it turned out *they've* felt belittled by you, too – but you didn't want to hear that. No – it was all my fault, for 'over-reacting'."

"It wasn't said with malice," he muttered. "I thought you'd realize that."

"Perhaps not – but why does any of it *matter*, Alan? The veg was over-cooked – so what? There's dust on the fireplace – is it really the end of the world? It's always so much worse when you're stressed; and at times, I can't help but wonder if finding fault gives you some sort of lift?"

"Look," he said. "We've talked before, about why I have high standards – you should know it's not about bringing anyone down. I just don't believe in doing half a job, whatever the task in hand – if you're going to do something, do it *properly*. And no doubt Barbara thinks I'm a chauvinist, but if *I* was the one who found myself at home, for some reason, it's no more than I'd expect of myself."

"It *is* done properly, though. I spend hours on it – yet you're always telling me I'm 'falling down on the job.' It really hurts."

"Oh, darling, that's all meant in *jest*, for heaven's sake! And of course, I *know* how thorough you are – but there's always room for improvement. I've been told many times I can be a hard taskmaster - but it gets results."

"At work, perhaps – but this is home; and maybe I want a husband, not a boss."

He didn't know what to say to that; it really seemed to stump him.

"You know," he said, after a moment or so, "I had an interesting conversation with Mark Quinn last week – he's just taken over as head of Claims. He worked under me a few years back, and I knew the guy couldn't stand me – but that comes with the territory, I'm afraid. You're not there to be liked! I often had words with him about deadlines – he did get there, but always by the skin of his teeth. It's not late, he'd say, so what's the problem? But if it was early, I said, you'd have more time to work on the next project, and do that even better. But he couldn't see where I was coming from.

"Anyway, I sent him on a course for time-management. He was furious! There was *nothing* wrong with his time-management, he said – and I was just looking for faults. Out to get him, were his exact words, I believe – but nothing was further than the truth. Perhaps we didn't get along, but I saw massive potential in Quinn – and if he could just brush up on a couple of things, he had it in him to be brilliant. And as much as he didn't like it, it all paid off. 'Look, Murdoch,' he said to me last week, 'I know we didn't see eye to eye, but thanks for everything. I learnt a lot from that course, and I think it helped with my promotion.' So, my point is, the easy route isn't always the best one."

"Okay," I said. "But how does that work for me? What do *I* get promoted to? Chief cook and bottle-washer? Because last time I checked, I was that already!"

Again, he seemed lost for words.

"Call me cynical," I went on, "but I suppose it all reflects well on you, doesn't it - when you have to entertain? Like with Fred – all that stuff about his wife being such a great cook, so I'd have to 'deliver', as you put it. Good job I didn't ruin the veg *then*, eh? After all, you got the promotion you wanted – I must have done *something* right!"

"That promotion was for all of us," he said. "Not just me. I thought you'd be pleased – better holidays, more often… Put it this way, I couldn't have stretched to that cruise without it."

And yes, the cruise was wonderful. Just the two of us; Mum and Dad sometimes took Dan away with them, and it turned out our trip clashed with their fortnight in Spain. I told Dan I was sure Nan and Grandad would understand if he cancelled, but he was adamant he was still going - and now I understood why. We had three weeks around the Bahamas, Barbados, Antigua, St Lucia – a luxury cabin, with an ultimate drinks and dining package… and best of all, Alan was relaxed. It was one of those times I thought we'd make it – but when we got home, it was back to square-one.

"The thing I loved about that trip," I said, "was that I felt like your wife, not one of your underlings. And of course, the cruise was fantastic – but I'd gladly swap it for a week at Butlins, if it meant things could be like that at home."

It still went completely over his head. "But what's the point of making do with second-rate? I want the best for us, Wendy – is that so wrong?"

"If it makes us unhappy, then yeah – I'd say it is." I paused. "And the thing is, Alan, it's not just me – it's Dan, with all this stuff about the Maths."

"You know how much I think of Dan," he said. "I just want him to make the most of his opportunities. I do push him, but it's kindly meant."

"So, threatening to send him to some boot-camp – you think *that's* kind?"

"Now, hang on," he blustered, "he must have taken *something* the wrong way, because there's no way I'd …. Oh, shit!" His face dropped. "It was that day, wasn't it? When your father was ill?"

"Yeah," I nodded. "Of all times."

"Shit!" His voice cracked again. "I thought he'd know I didn't *mean* it! Honestly, Wendy, it was just said in the heat of the moment. The way he spoke to me that evening was uncalled-for, and I was already at the end of my tether, after the day I'd had."

"Well," I said drily, "seeing Dan nearly lost his grandad, I don't suppose *his* day was great, either."

"I know - and all I was trying to do was help him to see the bright side – that at least his grandad was still here, and some mightn't be so lucky. And that, as hard at it is, this is an unfortunate part of life - and you have to try, somehow, to get on with it. Then he just swore at me, from nowhere, and I suppose it took me aback – it was so out of character. And I just wanted him to see that there are *consequences* for that behaviour."

"But why so *extreme*? Could you not just have said you'd ground him?"

"Okay." He sighed again. "Perhaps I *did* go a bit far. But I didn't think, for one minute, that he'd take me seriously!"

"You know," I said, "if it was just about the swearing, I might understand. And to be fair, I did have a go at him for that – tore a strip off him, in fact. But you *had* to make it about the Maths, didn't you?"

"No – no, I do think he may have misunderstood me there. I only mentioned that because I thought it might be a good chance to talk to him – about his attitude in general, and how he could improve."

"A chance to scare the hell out of him, more like! And it wasn't a one-off – he said you kept reminding him of it, every time you checked his homework."

"I only meant, remember what I'd said, about applying himself… And he thought…?"

"Yes – that if he didn't start getting A's, he'd be packed off to - well, it sounded like a sort of reform school. 'Approved schools', he said you called them."

"Only to shock him," he said sadly – and in fairness to him, I could see he genuinely felt awful. "That one time. I thought he'd have forgotten it."

"Well," I said, "clearly not. He only realized you were bluffing when he asked a teacher about them, and why kids got sent there. Don't worry – he didn't mention you. But safe to say, you're not his favourite person."

"I'll talk to the lad. Try and put things right. And look, Wendy, whatever my faults, I hope you know this wasn't intentional."

"For what it's worth, I believe you," I said. "But it might never have got that far, if you hadn't hounded him about his grades."

"I wasn't *hounding* him, for god's sake!"

"Oh, come on – you're *always* on about it! And he's not even doing badly! But the other thing is, perhaps he wouldn't have spoken to you like that, if you'd shown a *jot* of understanding about his grandad. Because I'll be honest, Alan, *I* felt like swearing at you that day, too! Yes, Dad was fine in the end, but it could easily have gone the other way – and you just seemed to brush that aside."

"As I said, I was trying to be optimistic - that's all."

"And making an impression on Fred the next day had *nothing* to do with it? As usual, it all came down to work – and I think that's the problem."

"You always knew I was ambitious, Wendy – I never made any bones of that."

"I just didn't think it would take over your life like this. And you asked me, before, what you'd done wrong. I tried telling you, twice, that sometimes I feel almost like someone who *works* for you, not someone you love. Both times, you ignored me and kept going on about your way being the best way. Perhaps none of it would bother someone less sensitive – but I can't change, any more than you can."

We fell silent for a while, as I took down the last of the posters.

"So," he said quietly, at last. "I guess that's it. It's not going to work, is it?"

"No." I smiled sadly. "I don't think it can."

Chapter Sixteen

And for a long time – five years or more – there was no-one else. Just me and Dan – the only man in my life, and that was how I wanted it. But then he left; and so much else has changed. There *is* someone now, and he makes me happy. As happy as I *can* be, without my boy….

"Smile". [iii]*"Put on a Happy Face"*. [iv]*"Keep your Sunny Side Up"*. [v]Song s I loved, growing up, but no-one tells you how bloody exhausting it is! And there's not much choice when you work with the public; perhaps that's why I cry so much in the shower.

But it's different this morning because *he's* here – my new man. I say "new" – it's been almost six months, now, but it doesn't feel anywhere near it. The time's gone so quickly, and I guess it does still feel strange – in a good way – after being on my own for so long. Of course, the sadness never goes away – but with him, I'm not *just* sad. And he gets that – after all, he's had enough hard times of his own.

So, no tears in the shower, today; standing together beneath that warm, soothing flow; wrapped tightly in those brawny arms as we kiss, deep and intense. We make love - slow, soft, sensual at first, gathering pace to a frenzied finish.

"Jesus, woman!" he growls playfully, with that warm, deep laugh. "I'm worn out, before the day's even started!"

"That's the idea," I smile. "No rest for the wicked!"

As we dress and dry, I enjoy his powerful physique, which you can tell has come from years of hard graft, not the gym – it's not perfectly sculpted, but tough and sinewy, with a few scars scattered here and there. There's a tattoo on his left upper-arm – the name of his first love, but I'm fine with that; we all have a past. His hair is thick and dark, and there's more of it on his face, and the rest of his body, than there is on his head.

Once dressed, we head through to the kitchen. I make a full-English, while he sets the table and gets some coffee on the go. He's not such a bad cook himself and has done a couple of meals for me round here. Not at his place, though, and I'd rather he didn't; it just wouldn't feel right, somehow…

It's getting on for 11, so it's more brunch than breakfast, really. We got back late last night, after my friend Angie's engagement party at Wavertree Town Hall. It was a lovely evening, and I'm made up for Ange, because I think, for a long time, she'd given up on anything like this happening for her. Not that it's the be-all-and-end-all, of course – but she'd spent years looking after her disabled parents and put her own life on hold. She was devastated to lose them, as you can imagine, but once she'd got through the worse, I think she saw it was *her* time now. Her fiancé, Paul, had been in a similar position – although in his case, it was a cantankerous old uncle he'd taken pity on, because no-one else in the family wanted to know.

I've worked with Ange for about four years, now. Despite being out of the civil service for so long, I got taken on again – I had to sit a re-entry test, and re-train, of course – it's changed quite a bit since the 60s! I'm back in a Jobcentre, and was signing people on at first, but then I took some 'A' levels and got promoted to Advisor. I can't say it's always an *easy* job; especially now, the way things are with unemployment, and morale being so low - but it's rewarding, and I really enjoy it.

Anyway, there were quite a few from the office there last night. I hadn't told any of them I'd met someone (didn't want to tempt fate – you know how I am for worrying!), so they were quite surprised, and really pleased for me. Ange remarked on how lovely he is – adding that it would soon be our turn to do this. And it hopefully will – but, for now, we're taking each day as it comes, and it's working out all the better.

It was after 1 when we got back, so we slept in a bit later this morning. We'd been thinking of going out for Sunday lunch over the water – this olde-worlde country pub in Thornton Hough (the Seven Stars, I think it's called), but it's a bit late for that now. We'll still head out for a drive, though; perhaps stop off for tea on the way back, but we'll just see how the mood takes us.

As we eat, we have the radio on in the background – Radio City Sunday Requests. We both smile wistfully as the Stylistics' "*You Make Me Feel Brand New*" [vi][vii] comes on. It's bitter-sweet – the words remind us of how we feel about each other, but we can't help but feel sad, too; it was one of her favourites.

"I'm sorry, love." He blinks back the tears. "It's mad, the way you can be happy and sad like this, all at once."

"Not at all," I say. "And don't be sorry – it makes perfect sense to me."

"Going back a couple of years, I never thought I'd smile again, but I am, Wend – and that's all down to you." He sighs. "And yet, at times, there's these little reminders – and I still can't believe she's gone! But you know it doesn't mean I'd change what *we've* got?"

"Of course, love. Because…look, it's not that I'm comparing the two in any way. I'd never want you to think that - it's far worse for you. I mean, at least I know he's safe and well, and his dad keeps me up to date. But it's just that thing, where so much in your life's going well – couldn't be better, in fact – but at the same time, you miss someone so much it hurts."

"Come here," he says. He hugs me tight, and we hold each other as the song plays out. "And it *is* as bad for you. You're the lad's mother! But give it time – he'll come round, in the end."

"Let's hope so, Bill. Let's hope so."

Chapter Seventeen

That's right – if you hadn't guessed already, it's Bill. I know – and, believe me, I've done a whole lot of soul-searching. We both have; but, in our heart-of-hearts, we know it's right – and what she'd want, too.

It's been almost three years since we lost Barb. The tail-end of 1982, not long before Christmas, and six weeks before Em's 16th, God love her. I could go on about how young she was; how unfair it was; that it was such a tragic waste; that she left a huge hole in everyone's lives. All those things people say – but it could never do it justice. Because Barb was *full* of life – warm, vibrant, creative energy – and how could *that* be gone? I always had my doubts about the afterlife, but now I'm convinced there *must* be something. Or else, where would it go? It can't just *disappear*!

She'd only been teaching for three years. She qualified in 1979, four or five months after I left Alan. She was brilliant at it, which was no surprise, and loved it even more than she'd expected. The more she got into it, the more creative she seemed to get, and she'd started writing poetry, too. Her gorgeous girl; a man who adored her; so much to give. "Unfair" didn't begin to come close.

And I think that's why I struggled, at first – with the guilt about being with Bill; as if I'd gained from her death. Because, the more unhappy I'd felt in my own marriage, I'd think, what *I'd* give for what they've got. But that wasn't meant begrudgingly; I just wished I could find it for myself.

I'll admit, I always found Bill attractive – and by that, I mean for who he was, not just looks. But it was in a way where I wanted Alan to be more like him – not where I wanted him for me! Sometimes, when the four of us were together, I'd look at Alan and think, if you were half the man your friend is…The thing is, though, I *knew* it was there in him. They'd grown up together after all, and from the sound of it, they weren't so different as kids. As they shared stories of the laughs they'd had, the scrapes they'd got into, Alan would relax and forget to be pompous – like he did on holiday, or when we were dating; or in bed…and if I could *just* get that warmth to come out more often, perhaps we could come close to Bill and Barb…. Then, after we parted ways, I often thought it would be nice to find a "Bill" of my own; but I was scared to take the risk, in case I got it wrong again, and how that would affect Dan

It was only after Barb died, and Bill and I grew closer, that I started thinking of him in that way – but I wouldn't let myself go there. Convinced as I was that Barb was still around, I thought she'd see it as the ultimate betrayal. I just had to be the best friend I could to him.

Even now, I still struggle to make sense of what happened to Barb. She was never ill, apart from those headaches – but, as time went on, they started getting worse. One day – around August '81, not long after the Royal wedding – she decided to see her GP, because the pain had been that intense, and a couple of times she'd been close to passing out. Best do some tests, the doctor said, just to rule things out; she kept it light, but I knew she was worried. Within days, she was called back to the surgery, to be told she was being rushed in for a biopsy – the scan had shown a tumour, which had most likely been growing slowly for the past few years.

It turned out benign, and we thought that would be an end to it. The operation to remove it went well; there was a tiny bit left, because of where it was located – they'd have to monitor that, they said, but she should make a full recovery. All was fine for almost a year; but then I had them round one night for dinner, and noticed her wincing again…

The part of the tumour they couldn't remove had turned malignant. It had spread fast, and there was nothing they could do. She was given three to six months, and was gone in five. 19th December, 1982, at 38; just a few years younger than her mum, when she'd died of the same thing. I'd say, for all of us, there was some relief mixed in with the heartache. We'd all grieved terribly while she was still here – it was so horrible, seeing her suffer like that, and knowing there wasn't a thing we could do.

"I think she always knew, you know," Bill said afterwards. "Because of what happened to her Ma. Right back when she first got those tests done, she kept saying she'd be fine, but I could see it in her – how scared she was…." His voice broke as he tailed off, but then, "I can't get like this," he muttered. "I need to be there for Em."

"Look, Bill," I said. "You'll be a rock for Em – just like you've been for Barb, through all of this But you're allowed not to be okay, you know, love. And I'm here if you need me."

"Thanks, Wend," he nodded. "It's appreciated."

But still, he went on, forcing himself to be strong – and all I could do was keep an eye on him. I had them both round for Christmas, which was as awful as expected – but at least we were all there for each other. The funeral, as you'd imagine, was devastating; but, at the same time, Bill did her proud, and it was just the kind of send-off I knew she'd love. And then, the next hurdle, at the end of January – Em's 16th.

I wouldn't have blamed the poor girl if she'd wanted to spend it in her room, and forget the day even existed. But throughout everything, she was so brave. Not in a way where she kept it in, like her dad; she cried when she needed to, but mixed in with this was lots of laughter, remembering their happiest times and those zany, madcap "Barb moments" we all loved. Her mum was really shining through in her; and for all our sadness, that brought a lot of joy.

So, when the big day came around, she was determined to mark the occasion. And what better way, she decided, than to make it a joint celebration – her mum's life, as well as her own coming of age? A big party wouldn't have felt right, of course – but a small gathering of family and close friends seemed ideal. The day itself was a school day (on top of everything, she was taking her 'O' levels - God knows how she got through them!), so she chose the Sunday after it for the get-together.

Dan and I got there just after 2.30; Barb's brother Richie was already there with their dad, Hugh. Richie was, as I expected, a male version of his sister - small, red-haired and full of fun. Poor Hugh, though, was a broken man – after all, he'd already gone through this with his wife. He'd been retired a couple of years, so must have been 67, maybe 68, but seemed much older; tough and wiry from working on the docks, but he looked vulnerable – almost frail. They didn't stay too long – I think Richie could see his dad was struggling.

Bill's brother, Roy, lives near London and his sister, Jennie, in North Wales; they couldn't make it, but there were plans afoot to visit them in Spring. Both of their parents had now passed away; their father in the early 70s (a month apart from John Murdoch), their mother in June '81. Poor Bill was still dealing with his grief over that - not to mention the estate, funeral costs and everything else - when Barb first took bad. Em had six of her close friends there, a mix of lads and girls, and they seemed a good bunch who rallied round her. Dan hadn't met them before, but fitted in well; as always, the love of music brought everyone together.

This was my first time round there since Barb had gone. It's a lovely house – a 3-bed semi off Brodie Avenue, towards the Garston end – and you could tell Bill had put a huge amount of work into it, over the years. As you might expect of Barb, the décor was bright, full of colour and a little off-the-wall. It was a strange feeling, being back there – those reminders hurt so much, yet brought so much comfort… A bit like crying in the shower, I guess….

Bill had put on a fantastic spread – Em had wanted to help, but he wouldn't hear of it. Once Hugh and Richie had left, he started clearing up, briskly, with that purposeful way of his, while the kids moved into the lounge and put their music on. I'll give Bill a hand in the kitchen, I thought – and found him, slumped and sobbing at the table.

I held him for a good ten minutes, maybe more, as he finally let it out. "You were right, Wend," he said at last. "I couldn't have kept on like that much longer. I just wanted to get Em through today, and she's done brilliant – I'm proud of her."

"No wonder, love," I said. "She's a credit to you both."

"You know, just watching here there, with her mates – it could just be her Ma." He filled up again. "Sorry," he muttered.

"Don't be!" I smiled. "This is what you need! I mean, I'm upset enough myself, and if *I'm* feeling like that…. Well, I can't begin to imagine…"

"To be honest, love," he said, "If it wasn't for Em, I'm not sure I'd still be here. I don't sleep – can't let myself. I just know I'll wake up, and there'll be that split second, before it all comes back…What will I do without her, Wend? What the hell am I gonna do without her?!"

He got there slowly – bit by bit – and I think Barb's birthday, a few months after Em's, was a turning point for us all. It was awful – the hardest day yet – but perhaps that helped, in some way, because nothing that followed could be quite so bad. When Bill turned 40, he felt inspired by Em to find his own way to celebrate; just a quiet meal for the four of us – him and Em, me and Dan. It was sad, of course – no escaping that – but at the same time, there was that feeling of having faced the worst, which made it just a little less raw.

As for me… I'm still in touch with my friend Jean from St. Helens, and I've got some good mates in work – but no-one can come close to Barb. She and Bill gave me so much support when I left Alan - we stayed with them for about three months, with myself in the spare room, and Dan on a put-you-up in the lounge. But besides this, she really helped me believe I *could* make a go of things on my own. It was her (and Bill, of course) who encouraged me, not just to reapply for the Civil Service, but to take exams and go for the promotion – and to stop underselling myself.

Alan stayed in touch – although only by phone or letter. We never saw each other face-to-face again, and even though we don't live far from each other, I never bump into him. All I'll say is that the kind, decent side showed itself, and he always made sure we were okay. He paid the deposit on the flat we're in now – hated the idea of us being somewhere run-down; and besides, he added, it was the least he could do, as he felt dreadful over what happened with Dan. I never told Dan any of this; and looking back, I wish I had…

The house on Menlove was sold, and I know Alan moved to somewhere smaller, off Allerton Road, still not far from Calderstones. My flat is above a shop on Allerton Road itself, but at the opposite end, nearer Penny Lane. It's lovely – small but cozy, and the ideal size for just the two of us. The proceeds from Menlove were split between us, and Alan sends a cheque each month. "And if there's anything more you need," he writes, "you only have to ask. My best to Dan. A."

Chapter Eighteen

My anxiety had eased off for a while, but it spiraled again when Barb died. She had this way of putting things in perspective, and I could tell her anything. I'm not saying I stopped worrying completely – but she always managed to calm me down, without ever being dismissive. Although they were such opposites, Bill has the same quality; and even then, in the midst of his own grief, he was there for me. "You miss her too," he'd say – but I could never have burdened him.

Dan, by now, was coming up to 17, and had started clubbing with his mates. I worried myself sick about him. Not that I had anything against his pals - they were decent enough lads, especially Tim Trafford, although I was never so keen on Jason Stopforth. Good-looking boy, but *knew* it; tall and slender, fine-featured, reddish-blonde - fancied himself as a Bowie-lookalike, and I suppose there *was* a resemblance. He was polite enough, but always seemed a bit too full of himself for my liking; and I know how much it hurt Dan that he made a play for Lori, within weeks of them splitting up. But whatever I thought of Jay, he was never the real problem - it was other kids, and what they'd do when they saw how they were dressed. All it would take was them to run into a gang of thugs....

Dan always tried to reassure me that they'd be okay; that they were careful, and would never have hung out where the "scallies" went. But it was the coming home that bothered me, especially if they couldn't get a cab. Sometimes it was almost 4 o'clock, and I wouldn't bother going to bed; I knew I wouldn't sleep till he was in, so what was the point?

"You didn't have to wait up, Mum," he'd say – and I got the feeling he thought I was just doing it to make him feel guilty. He'd say it was safer to leave together, rather than come away early on his own, and I did get that. But why did it always have to be so *late*? Whenever I asked him that, it invariably ended in a row. I didn't understand, he'd say, and it started reminding me of Jan with Mum. But Dan was nothing like his auntie – he'd never been any trouble – so it had to be his mates. Jason, I wouldn't mind betting. When I tried to bring it up, he'd get defensive – wouldn't hear a word against Jay, and once even asked if I resented him having friends at all!

Then there was Lori. I didn't mean to interfere – I was just terrified of him being hurt, and that it might lead to him doing something stupid; and perhaps I was over-reacting, but you do hear of it…. Believe me, I *wanted* to like her; it was just…. a sullenness in her, I suppose. Not that she was ever rude; but I got it into my head that she didn't think much of me – and if she cared for Dan, like she was supposed to, shouldn't she be making an effort? I did everything I could do welcome her. I knew she didn't eat meat, so I made cheese and egg-mayo sandwiches. She didn't touch them.

"She's vegan, not veggie," Dan said later. "I did try and tell you."

I'd thought it was the same thing – my mistake. But, and perhaps I imagined it, she seemed to look at them with disgust, and that feeling was very familiar ... I'd make conversation, but it felt like I was getting nowhere – and she'd say no to everything I offered, even a cup of tea! There's no milk in it, I'd tell her, but that wasn't it; the caffeine was the problem.

"For God's sake!" I said once. "What *does* she like?" I didn't mean to sound so harsh, but I couldn't help myself.

"Leave her alone, Mum," Dan said. He sounded weary. "She's got stuff on her mind."

Perhaps she did, I thought – but that wasn't *my* fault. I knew her father had died recently, and of course I felt sorry for her – but look at Em, and she'd just lost her mum! And I realize now how unfair I was. Everyone's different, and I knew nothing about what happened to Lori's dad - or how much support she got from her family. But at the time – well, I suppose didn't mean to push me away, but that was how it felt - and I just hoped she didn't do the same to Dan….

Then I got in one night to find him shut in his room, the music blaring, and I *knew* things weren't right.

"You'll be glad to know we've split up," he said flatly.

"Oh love, of course I'm not *glad!*" I said, and it was true – I was gutted for him. Yes, I thought he could do better, but I'd hoped he'd see it for himself. "Why would you think that?"

"Well – it's not like you didn't make it obvious."

"And what's *that* supposed to mean? I was nothing but kind to that girl!"

"Forget it, Mum." He shook his head. "Just forget it."

Knowing how down he was, I was worried about how it would affect his exams. But, to my relief, it went the other way - he threw himself into his work, probably to distract himself. He seemed okay after a while – at least till Jay Stopforth started seeing Lori. To be fair, she was a free agent, and I guess the lad didn't think he was doing wrong; but it still seemed a bit shitty of him. He *must* have known how Dan felt when she dumped him - and talk about rubbing salt in the wound! The only upside was that I think Dan started to see Jay in a slightly different light, and to back off from him - I can't say I wasn't pleased.

Things started to settle down between the two of us, and I hoped he'd realize I was just looking out for him. Every so often, I'd think of how bitter he sounded when he first broke up with Lori – but he was upset, I thought; just lashing out. As for the other stuff – that was years ago now; we'd both moved on since then, so I never thought, for one minute, that it might be on his mind.

And I think that's because when I divorced Alan, I assumed Dan would *know* I'd listened. We didn't discuss it again, because – well, least said, soonest mended... I couldn't change anything and dragging it out might only make it worse. I'd done the right thing in the end; surely that's what mattered?

Clearly not. It was all down to Bill and Barb, he'd said, the day he walked out – nothing to do with *him*. And yes, they did play their part – but leaving only ever became a *real* option when I saw Dan was unhappy. I'd wanted to explain that; but he'd gone before I got the chance.

It all started with a row about Uni, just after he'd got his 'A' Level results. It threw me when he said he was going for Bristol – all along, his heart had been set on Manchester, and I couldn't understand the sudden change.

"Why so far?" I asked him

He sighed. "Because that's the whole point - and it's not *that* far, anyway!"

We paused to look again at his offers; Liverpool, Manchester, Bristol, Leeds.

"You know," I said at last, "you could really do worse than Liverpool ...."

"Not *this* again, Mum...!"

"Okay, keep your hair on! I know you've got this thing about living away. But what's wrong with Manchester? You were always so keen on it before."

"Because I've told you, Mum - I'm going to Bristol – and I've already accepted. Now, can we leave it alone?"

"But what if you're homesick?"

"Then I'd go to Dad and Sue's. They're not far away – and they said I can stay whenever I want."

"I see. So, you're fine to stay with them – but not with me?" I hated how childish that sounded, but I couldn't help myself. Perhaps his dad had put the idea in his head. Brian's fault, *again*...!

"Look, Mum," Dan said wearily. "My mind's made up. You'll just have to accept it."

I wiped my eyes. "Well - anyone would think you were desperate to get away from me!"

No response.

"And they'd be right – wouldn't they?"

He shrugged.

"But why, son? I don't get it! You've got a lovely home…"

"…and I'm so *ungrateful* – I know! It's the same spiel I got when you were with Alan."

Then it all came out – not just about Alan, but everything else, even as far back as Philip and Peter. And Lori, of course. She only ended it because of me, he said; because she knew I didn't like her.

"I didn't *dislike* her," I tried to say. "I just thought she could have made more effort. I was always friendly, but I stopped bothering in the end – it felt too much like hard work!

"You've got no idea what she's been through, Mum - and not just because she lost her dad."

"I'm not a mind-reader, Dan – why didn't you tell me?"

"Because you don't *listen*!" he yelled. "You *never listen*! It's always the same old story – *talk* to me, son – tell me what's on your mind. But when I do..." He laughed bitterly. "I tried telling you about Phil and Peter's mum – you just ignored me. Then the way you tore into me when I told you about Alan...."

"That was a mistake, love." What else could I say? "The whole thing was a mistake. I should never have married him. But at least I did something about it, in the end."

"Yeah - thanks to Bill and Barb. You didn't want to hear it from me! You make a big deal over nothing, then keep going on and on that it's only because you care – because you *worry* about me! But then, when it really *matters*..."

"Please don't do this, Dan. If I could only go back in time..."

"But you can't, can you?" He paused. "And the more I think about it, maybe I should leave now – tonight."

I sighed. "Look, I know you're not happy, but it doesn't have to come to that. Surely we can sort this out…"

"At the moment, Mum…I'm not sure I want to."

"Oh, love, come *on*…"

"I'm going to stay with Dad, before the term starts – then hopefully get a place in Halls."

He stormed off to his room to pack. I followed him in, and it was like a re-run of when I left Alan – but this time, it was my turn to sit on the edge of the bed, trying to convince him he didn't *really* want to go through with it.

"Listen," I said, "If you're just doing this to punish me.... well, I already know I let you down."

"I'm not punishing anyone. I just need some space, that's all."

"Okay - if it's got to be Bristol, that's fair enough. I won't stand in your way. But you've got a few weeks yet. Does it really have to be *now*?"

"Yeah," he muttered. "The sooner the better."

And then - well, you know the rest.

I lost track of time after that. It can be so draining, that constant brave face - and I spent the weekends sleeping; or crying.

"I know he won't want to speak to me," I said to Brian on the phone, "so don't try to put him on. But please talk to him, Bri."

"I'll do my best, love. And look – I don't know what's gone on between you, but you know what they're like at that age. He'll see sense."

"I'm not so sure," I said tearfully. "I think – well, I know – it's to do with Alan."

"Really?" Brian sounded quite shocked at this, which surprised me; I thought Dan would have told him everything. "I mean, I'll be honest, I was never struck on the guy – he seemed too far up his own arse. But I thought Dan got on alright with him?"

"So did I – until he started pressuring him about his grades. And before you say it, I know – you warned me about that, and I was having none of it."

"That's all in the past now, Wend – and I've never been one for grudges."

"Thanks, Bri – as long as you know, I did see it, in the end. That's why I got out - but I don't think Dan knows... So just tell him I'm on his side, hon, that's all I ask."

I put the phone down, and it rang again, straightaway.

"Wend?" Bill said. "Are you alright, love? I've been worried."

"Oh, Bill – I'm so sorry!" I felt awful. I'd either seen him or spoken to him most weekends since Barb died, just to check in; but it must have been at least three weeks…

"Look, don't be daft," he said. "I was just making sure all was okay. And it's not – is it?"

"Don't worry, Bill – I'm fine – it's something and nothing…"

"I'm coming over."

"No…no, Bill – I don't want to put you out."

"Put me out? The way you've been there for me and Em? I'll be there in a bit. No arguments."

And he was – and it all went from there. We talked for hours – then kissed – then ended up in bed. It seemed like the most natural thing in the world, and I'd never felt so safe – yet, at the same time, so wracked with guilt over Barb. It all changed, though, once we told Em.

"About bloody time!" she laughed. "I was wondering when you'd get your acts together!"

"And you're sure it's okay, Em?" I asked. "Because the last thing I'd want to do is disrespect your mum."

"Look," she smiled. "Do you honestly think that woman would want either of you unhappy? She'll be cheering you on!"

Of course, we both have our wobbles – like this morning, when that song was on – but we get through them. After the Stylistics comes Dr Hook's "*A Little Bit More*", [viii]which is one Bill loves, and cheers us both up; and that sets us back on track for the day.

As we clear away the dishes, it just comes to me – best check the answerphone – I haven't had it long, and I always forget…

One new message. "Mum…?"

"You see?" Bill smiles. "What was I saying?"

"Mum…?" My heart leaps as I hear my boy's voice, then drops at once; he sounds so broken. "It's Dad… I think he's dying.

Dan

Chapter Nineteen

The answerphone threw me. It must be new – we never had one when I was last there, and because I wasn't expecting it, I thought it was *her*. "Hi, Mum," I started – but then her voice carried on. "This is Wendy. Can't get to the phone right now..."

I hadn't meant to blurt it out like that, and if I'd spoken to her properly... well, who knows? I might still have done the same. *He's dying* – that was all I could think of. They hadn't said that for *definite*, but they'd told us to prepare for the worst – and the look on that doctor's face; I just knew it must be bad... really bad....

I put down the phone, knowing she'd panic when she heard it. It might have been a long time since they'd split up, but they stayed good mates – she'll be gutted if the worst happens, I thought. I walked back along the corridor, to the where Sue was in the waiting-room. Apart from the stark white walls, everything in there was blue – floor, seats, even the leaflets on the table. Nothing to relieve it, save a poster of a bright red apple, headed "7 Steps to a Healthy You", which Sue was studying intently. Nothing usually phases Sue. She's tall, slim, classy, and what Mum might call "no-nonsense", but lovely with it. That day was the first time I'd seen her cry, and she looked completely done-in.

"Quit smoking," she muttered, still scrutinizing the poster. "More fruit and veg. Less red meat. Less booze. Well, I tell you one thing – when I get him home, there'll be changes!" She smiled at me, wearily. "Anyway, sweetheart – did you manage to get hold of your mum?"

I shook my head. "Straight to answerphone. I left a message."

Sue glanced at her watch. "Well, it's getting late – she could be in bed. Try in the morning – by then, we should know..." She tailed off, close to tears again. "An ulcer – of all things! The most laid-back man anyone could meet... Oh, here we are..."

The doctor had just come out – the same one as before and looking even more serious.

"Well?" Sue asked him.

"Mrs. Cooper," he said, then paused a moment. "I'm afraid there were complications, Mrs. Cooper..."

That's it, I thought. He's gone. Fuck – what do I do now? He's gone – oh, *fuck*, he's *gone*.... I'll have to tell Mum... I'll have to be there for Sue, and Abby... and how *can* I, when *I* don't know what to do next...?

"If you're just doing this to punish me...." Mum said, the night I left home. I said no, but I was – of course I was... Dad told me, loads of times, that she'd spoken to him – how much she was missing me, and when was I going to get in touch? I'm not ready, I kept saying; I knew she was upset, but I wouldn't budge. When I last spoke to Dad, on Sunday, I said I'd think about it – that was nearly a week ago. I'd wanted to prove a point – so, yeah – I *was* trying to punish her. And now, *I* was the one being punished, for treating her like crap...

"You only get one Mum," Dad said last week. "Try and put things right, son, because you never know the minute." And I knew what he meant – look what happened to Barb! I remember what that was like for Em, and thinking, what if that was *my* mum? Then, when my mate Neil came into the shop, to tell me about the call... straight-off, I thought something had happened to her – and I should have listened to Dad. Didn't cross my mind it might be *him*....

.... So – what do I do now? I wondered. I'd only been this terrified once before. The time I thought I'd lost Grandad.

Chapter Twenty

It was a Friday, and I was due round there that night – and in some ways that made it worse. Because all day, I'd looked forward to seeing them both, and just getting a break – from everything. So, I was gutted to find I wasn't going after all. It had all been on, as usual, that morning; but then I get home from school and it's suddenly not happening – and she won't tell me why. Then I see she's been upset and get a really bad feeling....

I ask her what's wrong. Nothing, she says at first, but then, "Grandad had a bit of a shock.". What kind of shock? I ask, and she bursts into tears. She can hardly speak for crying – he's in hospital, is all I can make out. Then I get upset too, because I'm wondering just how ill he is... or even if he's dead... And in a few minutes, it's gone from not seeing him that night – to maybe not seeing him again.

Grandad's okay now, she says at last - but I'm not sure I'll believe it, until I see him for myself. But that didn't end up being till Sunday; because the next day we had this snobby couple round for dinner, and Mum was in the kitchen for hours. I can't remember their names – only that they were as dull as fuck. "*Really*?" Mum kept saying to them. "How *interesting*!" But I could tell she was bored shitless, like I was. Then, the longer it went on, I remember starting to feel down; because in twenty years or so, I thought (or maybe ten – I reckon that couple were younger than they looked), that's how just Mum and Alan would end up. I knew Mum was just going along with it all; but I felt like screaming at her, what are you *doing*, Mum? You're nothing like them – you're *cool* – *funny*!

And that was true – still is. She can't see it in herself, but when she's not worried or stressed, she's a right laugh. I know she and Dad rowed a lot, but when they got on, they were like a double-act. With Dad, it was a constant stream of one-liners, so everyone would think *he* was the funny one; but every so often, Mum would come out with a quip of her own, and it was hilarious. They both loved their music; mainly the Beatles, but Mum was into Fleetwood Mac, and Dad liked the Faces (and the Floyd, of course – the one thing he and Alan had in common). Looking back on those days, there were some good times – until Mum went off on one... I missed Dad when he first went; but it was the right thing, and I think I always knew that.

Chapter Twenty-one

They had these mates who lived a few doors down from us -
Jean and Eric Stack. Mum stayed in touch with Jean after we
moved – still speaks to her now, as far as I know. They were
okay – a bit "twee", Dad said, but no harm in them. Jean
seemed a throw-back to the early 60s and looked a bit like Mum
on her wedding photos, with her hair in a huge beehive. Eric
was an accountant, I think, or maybe worked in a bank; thin,
greying, mild-mannered, with horn-rimmed glasses - always in
the garden. Their son, Keith, was two or three years older than
me. He went to the same school, but our paths never crossed - I
was still in Infants at the time. He seemed shy, like his dad, and
was tall and skinny, with tight blonde curls and buck teeth.

Mum was quite close to Jean, back then – but although Dad got
on okay with Eric, they didn't have much in common, mainly
because of the age-difference. Jean was in her thirties; Eric at
least ten years older, maybe fifteen, so probably closer to
Grandad's age. The only music he liked was classical, and he was
more for the rugby than the footie. I think they went for a pint a
couple of times, but it was hard-going, Dad said- nice enough
bloke, but nothing to say. Mostly, Mum and Jean met up on
their own – lunch or shopping – but every now and then we'd
go round for a meal.

The first time I remember going (we may well have been before
that), we had dinner (roast beef, I think), then the mums sent
me and Keith off to play in his room. It was time, Jean said, for

"drinkie-poos". She put some music on – something MOR, like the Carpenters or Seekers – while I followed Keith upstairs; and I could tell straight-off he wasn't pleased.

The room was blue and yellow, and full of books and games. Some of them I had myself, some I'd not heard of, and one I'd have loved – Subbuteo™. Keith must have seen me eyeing it up, because he knocked me roughly away.

"Keep your hands *off!*" he growled. "I'm *warning* you!"

"Sorry…" I stammered. "But your mum said…"

"I don't care *what* Mum said. You're not going near them!"

"Sorry," I said again, tearfully. "I'll go back down…"

"No, you won't!" he snapped. "And you *dare* think about grassing! Now, just sit down, and stop whining – NOT on the bed! Over *there!*"

Then he played alone as I watched miserably from the floor. I couldn't have cared less about the games – it was the shock, I guess. He'd been so butter-wouldn't-melt at the table – meek and harmless, like his father. And I hadn't even *asked* to go in his room! All I wanted was to get out of there, but I was stuck – because, as Keith rightly guessed, there'd be questions if I went down in tears…

After a bit, we heard Jean on her way upstairs – "Just bringing you boys some drinks," she called chirpily.

"Get up," Keith ordered, under his breath, "and stop snivelling! And I mean it – say one word, and you're dead!"

I got hastily to my feet, drying my eyes, and he shoved me towards the Subbuteo, to make it look like we were playing it together.

"*Here* we are!" Jean smiled, as she came in with two tall glasses of lemonade. "Enjoying the Subbuteo, Danny? Your mum tells me you want one for Christmas. Let's see what Santa brings, eh?"

"*Let's see what Santa brings!*" Keith sneered, once his mum was out of earshot. "I bet you still believe, don't you, little baby…. Give that *here!*"

I was about to take a swig of the lemonade, but he snatched it off me, downing both glasses in one go. Then, grabbing my arm, he gave me what I now know is a Chinese burn – all I knew back then was that it hurt like fuck. He covered my mouth to stop me screaming.

"And that's nothing," he smirked, "to what you'll get if you tell – d'you hear me?"

I nodded. Good, he said – because he had a big gang of "dead hard" mates, who'd "get" me after school if I said anything. And his Auntie Brenda had a friend who was a witch, and could easily turn me into a spider…

… It happened three or four times after that. Of course, I knew it was bullshit about the witch – and he shot himself in the foot by saying she'd give me Turkish Delight, before turning me to stone. He had all the *"Narnia"*[ix] books, I noticed; mustn't have crossed his mind that I might have read them too.

"Like Mr. Tumnus?"[x] I asked.

His face dropped. "Shut it," he said sullenly. "I'm just saying watch it, that's all."

As for the gang – it may have been true, maybe not, but that wasn't the point. I wasn't scared of the threats. I just hated going there; being forced to hang out with someone who treated me like crap, and seemed to get such a kick from being vile to younger kids. It felt like the mums were pushing us together because *they* were friends – and even if Keith had been okay, I didn't like that. I had mates of my own.

"Are you okay, love?" Mum asked one day, just after we'd been. "You've been very quiet."

Next is, I'm telling her everything; she looks upset at first – then angry.

"Look, Danny," she said sternly, at last, "you'd best not be fibbing over this. Because Jean and Eric are really good friends – and if I say something to them, and it turns out you're making it up…"

"Don't say anything, Mum," I said desperately – because I knew how it would go. My word against his - then Mum would fall out with Jean, and it would all be *my* fault. I didn't *want* her to tell them – just to stop taking me round there.

"Why not?" she demanded.

I looked at the floor. "Dunno."

She sighed. "It's because it's not true – isn't it?"

I nodded. What was the point? They'd think I was lying anyway.
Then she starts screaming at me, the way she used to with Dad.
She'd never been that way with me before, and never was again
– not until that other time, years later…

Why did I do it? she kept shouting. What was *wrong* with me?
Why, why, why? I just don't like him, I said in the end, and she
flew at me even more. I could have got poor Keith into a lot of
trouble – and he was a nice, quiet boy – what could I possibly
have against him? It wasn't like me to be so unkind, she added,
but any more of it, and I could forget that Subbuteo I wanted.
It's okay, I said flatly - I'd gone off it anyway.

She was off with me for the next few days, but then it all blew
over – and I did notice that we never went again, and she stuck
to seeing Jean on her own. I moved to Juniors the next year, and
never saw Keith around; except this one time when some lads
were laying into him, and I wondered if *they* were the "hard
mates" he'd threatened me with.

Chapter Twenty-two

By the time we moved to the estate, I'd completely forgotten it; never thought of it for years, not until I left home. But it must have been there, somewhere; because when I changed schools and the bullying started, the one thing I knew was that I couldn't tell Mum – or anyone.

Even now, I don't like talking, or even thinking about it. I know Mum had her suspicions, but it was much worse than she could have guessed. It only lasted for two, maybe three months, but in that time – it might sound mad, but it was almost like I wasn't the same kid! Apart from Keith Stack, I'd never been picked on before – never not had friends. I guess I was always a bit shy with strangers, but not when I was with my mates; and I'd loved school - been really happy. Then to go from that, to being terrified… and it didn't help that I missed Dad.

It got to the point where I dreaded waking up. I knew Mum's grandad had died in his sleep, and that's what I wanted for me. When it didn't happen, I thought of other ideas – perhaps I'd run out in the road, not watching where I was going…but I couldn't have done that to Mum and Dad. I could bunk off, but I knew I'd never get away with it – and Mum was bound to guess if I said I was ill. If I ran away, they'd be worried sick – and anyway, where would I go? Dad's place was obvious – but of course, he'd have to let Mum know, and she'd bring me back, and it would all come out…

I wasn't sure if I believed in God, but I started praying last thing at night, for something – *anything* – to change and make it stop, or even just get easier. Just *one* mate who was on my side… I'd more or less given up hope – but then, when things were pretty much at their worst, there was Phil.

A few of them – Wayne Watkins, Stephen Dee, Arnold Molyneux, and a couple of others - had stuck me in the bin. Each time I tried to get out, they'd shove me back down, then throw more stuff on top of me – litter, mainly, but in the past, there'd been soil, or even dogshit.

"Go on, Mummy's Little Boy," Wayne sneered. "Cry – *cry!*"

The others stood round laughing – "mummy's boy, mummy's boy!" – and not for the first time, I wished Mum had taken notice when I said I didn't need picking up from school…

…Then, next is, Phil's dragging me out of the bin, and punching Watkins in the face. He tried to go for the others, but they'd run off already. Then Watkins starts whining, and our form teacher, Mrs. Crick, marches Phil off to the Head.

I felt bad over that. The Head, Mr. Jackson – known to all as "Jake" - he seemed okay but was cane-happy with lads he didn't like. Phil was his main scapegoat- and Peter, at times, probably just for being Phil's brother. Mrs. Crick was just the same. I couldn't stand her – a smug, sarcastic woman with black hair and loads of freckles. Always telling Phil that he'd amount to nothing – then wondered why he had an "attitude problem", as she called it.

So, I went to wait for Phil outside Jake's office. Peter was there too but didn't speak – just sat with his head down, poor lad; scared of his own shadow, even more than *I* was in that place.

After a while, Phil comes out, rubbing his hands together, and trying his best not to cry. I tell him I'm sorry I got him into trouble, and he says, don't worry, lad – Watkins had it coming – and why don't I hang out with them?

Phil was nothing like the friends I had in Windle, or the ones I had in Liverpool, later on – but he was one of the best mates I'd ever had. As I got to know him (and Peter, as much as I could), I realized how shit their life was at home – their mum was an alcoholic, who completely neglected them. The teachers looked down on them both, when they should have looked *out* for them, and that really got Phil's back up. He wasted no time in telling them what he thought, and it was this that got him branded as trouble.

Watkins and his gang never touched me after that – just shouted abuse from afar. They ridiculed Phil and Pete for being scruffy, and because Phil was into heavy rock - but they were scared of him, too, and made sure they were at a far enough distance to get away. I can't say I was ever *happy* in that place; I still missed Dad, and my old life. But at least I felt safe now, and not like I didn't want to be here at all – and that was all down to Phil.

I don't think Mum knew this, but it was *me* who told them to come round whenever they wanted – because, when I thought of how bad their life was, and what Phil had done for me…. *I* was the one who put the idea in their heads, that one day Mum might take them in – maybe even adopt them. Pipe-dreams- I can see that now; but I was stupid and naïve enough at the time to think I could really make it happen.

Mum seemed fine with it at first – often said she felt sorry for the lads because they seemed "unloved." I mentioned they'd been happy at their nan and grandad's, and at one point she even tried to look their number up. She was pleased they enjoyed her cooking – "those poor lads," I heard her say to Nan, "at least they get *one* good meal a day…" But I noticed a change when she got with Alan. Perhaps it was down to him – he was always going on that she "needed to be firmer." But it was around that time that I started going to Nan's on a Friday, when she and Alan were out. Mum told the lads not to call on those nights – but when she was out of earshot, I said to come anyway, and pretend they'd forgotten – in the hope that, with any luck, she'd let them tag along.

"I did tell you boys we were going out," she said – not angrily, but definitely letting them know the score. Their faces dropped, and I felt awful; but when I opened my mouth to say it was my fault, Phil shook his head. It's alright, he mouthed - no worries. Then, "Sorry, Mrs. C. I just forgot."

Things settled down again, after a bit – until she bumped into their mum. I was with Nan and Grandad that day, so I'm not sure where it was, or what happened – only that Mum thought she was rude and making a fool of her. I remember thinking, now she *knows* how bad their mum is, doesn't that mean we should be doing more? I tried to suggest that, but she just smiled. I had a good heart, she said; she was proud of that – but I had to realize that I couldn't fix everything. Then, that night she turned them away – no wonder Phil got upset. Mum thought I was in tears because he swore - but it was because I knew it was my fault; and that's what I got, for promising the world.

When I look back, I know it's true, what she said; that some things are out of your hands - and, as hard as you try, you *can't* put them right. Even if Mum *hadn't* been marrying Alan, or planning to move back to Liverpool, I doubt she could have taken those lads in – if she'd rung Social Services, they'd have gone into care. What I'd been trying to say was that I'd ask Phil for his nan's address – so Mum could go and speak to them, like she'd wanted to before – but she shut me down, before I had the chance. Perhaps she hadn't meant to, but that's how it felt. Like she wasn't really *listening* - because she'd already decided there was nothing she could do; and that it wasn't our problem, anyway.

Chapter Twenty-three

For the record, I don't hate Alan. I did for a while, but now –
I'm not saying we'd ever be best mates, or anything – but our
paths crossed a few years ago, and we made our peace.

Once we left, Mum never mentioned him. I had no idea if they
were in touch (but guessed they might be), or if he still lived on
Menlove. Then, one Saturday (I think it was just before Barb
was ill), I bumped into him on Allerton Road, in the queue in
WH Smith's ™. Hadn't changed much – the 'tache had grown
out into a beard – a few more grey hairs, but that was it. I was
surprised he recognized me at all.…

"It's great to see you, Dan. How are things going?"

"Yeah," I said steadily, "not so bad."

"That's good to hear."

We only spoke for a few minutes. He asked about school. It was
fine, I said – told him we were getting ready for 'O' Levels next
year, and I still wanted to teach Art.

"Good… good," he said, then cleared his throat. Is he going to
start harping on about the Maths? I wondered – but then,
"Listen, Dan – before you left, there was – um – a
misunderstanding… And, well - I just want you to know, that if
I'd thought…"

"It's alright." You might be thinking I let him off too easy – but don't forget, a lot had changed since I last saw him. I know *I* had – and as for him… Don't get me wrong, he still seemed full of himself - but maybe slightly less than before.

"Good," he said again, and you could see the relief in his face. "I'm glad I ran into you, Dan, because it – well, it was playing on my mind." He smiled – a bit sadly, I thought. "Anyway – must fly. Best of luck with those exams."

Chapter Twenty-four

I'd got on fine with him at first. Not that he'd ever come close to Dad, of course. But he'd seemed okay; even a laugh, at times - especially when Bill was round, with all the stories of when they were kids.

Dad wasn't over-keen. He never said anything at the time – wanted me to make my own judgement, he told me later. But I once overheard Mum telling Nan that she "got the feeling Brian was jealous." Dad always *knew* she thought that and was laughing about it when I saw him last weekend.

"I mean, what's there to be jealous of? He just got up my nose, that's all – thinking he's better than me!"

That day was the first time I'd told Dad any of this. Not that I didn't *want* to. But I knew he and Mum spoke a lot on the phone, and if anything slipped out... well, on top of everything else, she'd be upset I'd turned to him and not her. Anyway – I'd been there for Sunday lunch, like I'd done most weekends since coming to Uni. Sue usually cooked, and me and Abs helped Dad with the dishes, but this time they'd swapped over. Dad did a pretty good job with the roast – leg of lamb with mint, roasties, cauli, garden peas, and plenty of gravy.

"Be warned," Sue said, "I could easily get used to this!"

Dad grinned. "Fine by me – anything to get out of the washing-up!"

Sue started clearing the table. "Why don't you boys go for a pint?"

"Aye-aye!" Dad laughed. "I think she's trying to get rid of us! But what d'you reckon, son? It's been ages since we had a Dad-and-Lad's day."

The pub was just up the road – one of those olde-worlde types with oak beams. It's nice, where Dad and Sue live, in Worle, just outside Weston; near enough to everything, but feels like you're out in the country.

"Listen," Dad said, once he'd got back from the bar, "I'll have to be upfront. We planned it this way, me and Sue – so you and me could have a talk."

I smiled. "Don't worry – I was already on to you."

"It's just this thing with your mum…"

"How did I guess…?"

"Look, lad – I dunno what's gone on between you, but it's breaking her heart, all this. Why not call her, at least?"

I sighed. "I'm just – not sure I'm ready."

Then he said that stuff about life being too short, and you only get one mum. "I just don't want you having regrets, son, that's all. And it doesn't seem worth it, over some stupid row."

"I know, Dad," I said. "It wasn't just the row, it's… It's hard to explain."

"She thinks it's to do with that bell-end she was married to."

I shrugged. "Yeah – I suppose that's part of it."

"She didn't tell me much – just that he'd piled the pressure on about your grades. For Christ's sake, I thought – you were nowhere *near* your exams at that time – but then, I'd always had an idea he'd be like that. I tried to warn her, when they first got together, but she wouldn't listen – she feels awful about that now."

"She *doesn't* listen, though, Dad – that's the problem."

"And that's why you got off?"

I nodded. "I can't talk to her. She's always saying to go to her if anything's up, but then as soon as I did…"

"Did you try telling her about *him?*"

"Yeah… It was just this thing he said to me, that time Grandad was ill. I mean, I suppose I should have known it was a bluff…"

"But that was a while ago, son - you were still only a kid." Dad sighed. "So – this thing he said…?"

"For a start, he just didn't *get* it over Grandad. Kept going on to Mum that she needed to pull herself together, and the more he said it, the more she got upset. It's mad, because he *loved* Mum – I could see that – but there were these other times when… I dunno, it was just the way he spoke to her. So, the more he harps on, in my head I start telling him to fuck off. Then later, when I'm doing my homework, he comes in and says we need a talk. 'You'll be 12 next month,' he says. 'Too old for all this crying over nothing – it really *has* to stop.' And I'm saying it again in my head – fuck off, fuck off, fuck off – then before I know it, it just comes out.

"He stands there, glaring, and I wonder what he'll do next. 'You're lucky I'm not my father,' he says at last. 'Because I know one thing - if *I'd* behaved like that, he'd have taken a belt to me. Now, I'm more of a man of *reason* than he was – but be warned, sonny - any more of it, and they have schools, out in Wales and the Lakes, for lads who are trouble.' Then he tells me they're called Approved Schools, and how tough they are – a bit like the army, but much worse, because after all, you're there as a punishment. And that he wouldn't *want* to send me to one... but if he didn't see an improvement in my attitude, it could easily be arranged.

"And I can see now, he was just trying to shock me. But he had this *way* of saying things – maybe it was how he spoke in work, but it sounded deadly serious; like he could really make it happen. So, I tried apologizing – said it was because I was worried about Grandad. But it wasn't just that, he said. He was fed up of me expecting everything on a plate – because he *knew* I could do better at Maths, but I just wasn't *trying*. Then, before he goes out, he says I'll need to pull my socks up – and be mindful of what he'd said.

"It settled down after that – I mean, he never mentioned those schools again, but it was always on my mind. And there were always those comments when he checked my homework.

'Remember that talk we had?' he'd say – and I got it into my head, that if I didn't start getting A's.... Well, I suppose I just put two and two together."

"No wonder!" Dad said angrily. "I *knew* that guy was a tosspot, but what the fuck...?!"

"In fairness, I ran into him a while back – and give him his due, he did apologize. I think he meant it."

Dad rolled his eyes. "Yeah, well – be sure and get that medal in the post, eh?" We laughed. "Call me a cynic, but it's always too easy, once the damage is done... So – did Mum know any of this?"

I shook my head. "Not at first. But then she said I wasn't myself, and... thing is, if she hadn't asked, I'd never have told her. I don't even know why I did – but I thought maybe she'd get it, because of how he was over Grandad.... But anyway, she just kicked off on me for swearing at him – said I was ungrateful, and I needed to suck it up and deal with it. It just ended up like every other time I'd told her stuff and wished I hadn't."

Dad sighed. "Look, son – I'm not defending how she reacted – but she must have listened in the end, because she did end up leaving."

"I know. That's what I thought, too. But when we stayed with Bill and Barb, I'd overhear her saying she'd never have done it, if it wasn't for them."

"Well, your mum always doubts herself. Perhaps they just gave her the push she needed. And she must have said something to *him* – for him to apologize."

He was right, of course. I'd never thought of it.

"Look," I said, "I'll speak to her. I promise."

"Good lad." Dad smiled, finishing off his pint. "Anyway – I'll get more drinks in."

I noticed him wince as he got up.

"You okay?" I asked.

"Yeah," he grinned. "Yeah… just a dodgy curry last night. Ordered Madras, but I'm sure it was Vindaloo - near blew me mouth off! But I'll be fine."

Chapter Twenty-five

If she'd just accepted I was going to Bristol, we might have been okay. But she wouldn't let it go; and the more she went on, the more I remembered why I wanted out in the first place....

That stuff with Alan was always on my mind, but it wasn't the *only* thing. For one, she tried to deny that she didn't like Lori, but I could tell, straight-off. "She's very *quiet*," she kept saying, as if that made her the world's worst (and yet she'd moan about my mates having too much to say!) I'd told her, more than once, what vegan meant, but she still made out she didn't know. Don't bother making anything to eat, I said, but she went ahead anyway – then complained about it going to waste! After all, it was vegetarian – so what was the problem? So, I explained – again - what vegan was....

"Well, I don't *remember* that!" she said indignantly. "And anyway – I've never heard of anything so silly! All these fads get on my nerves. They're lucky to get decent food! Your nan had to put up with rationing. It was still on when Auntie Jan and I were kids."

What could I say to that? Nan and Grandad had told me loads about the war – I knew how tough it was. I'd never have made light of it, even though people (like Mum!) thought the "youngsters" would never understand.

Lori never drank tea or coffee. Mum really seemed to take offense at that.

"Does she not think I'm good enough for her?" she asked one day. "Is *that* why she says no to everything?"

I shrugged. "She just doesn't like it."

Mum rolled her eyes. "So, is there anything she *does* like? Just watch yourself, son. I'm worried she'll end up hurting you."

"Why – because she doesn't drink tea?"

"She never seems very happy, that's all I'm saying. And I just hope this isn't one-sided."

She was right about her not being happy - but that was all because of her dad. I'd met her the year before, when they'd just started taking girls in the 6th Form. Only four of them – Rosie Darch, Emma Makin, Allie Spence and Dolores (Lori) Whitfield. Rosie was small, slim, white-blonde, and the one everyone fancied. Jay went out with her for a while; she made his life hell after he dumped her, but it was probably no more than he deserved. Of the four, Lori was easily the quietest; in fact, it was a month or more before she spoke to any of us. She'd come from the same school as the other three, but although she sat with them at lunch, you could tell she was on the outside. I'm not saying she was bullied, exactly, but there did see a bit of sniggering behind her back – and Jay was the worst.

"Give it a rest, lad," I said in the end. "What's she ever done to you?"

"You just want your leg-over," he smirked. "I mean, to be fair, she *is* a looker – but it's wasted on *her*."

Gobshite, I thought. I knew Mum had no time for him; and as much as I hated to admit it, I was starting to think she had a point.

It was true, though – I *was* into Lori, and had been from day-one. She was in my A-level Art group, and was brilliant, way ahead of the rest of us; and she looked – and dressed – a bit like Siouxsie Sioux. I spoke to her a few times in class but got nowhere at first - she thought Jay had put me up to it.

"Because I'm not stupid," she added. "I know he laughs at me."

I muttered something garbled about him being like that with everyone, but she didn't want to hear it.

"I just think you're in it together."

"No, Lori....I know he's my mate, but you've got this all wrong...."

"Look, just leave it, Dan – and leave me alone."

"Okay," I sighed. "But it's not what you think."

Next time we were in Art, I kept my distance. It was the last class that day, so I took my time packing up at the end - then I noticed she'd waited.

"Sorry I was off the other day," she said. "I've got stuff going on at home. And I know your mates think I'm weird – but that's why I don't feel like talking."

"*I* don't think you're weird."

Everyone had gone by now. We kissed, just for a few seconds; she looked taken-aback, but not in a bad way.

"Come on," I said.

It turned out she lived a few roads away. As we walked home through the park, she told me her dad had died six months earlier but had been ill for years. She never said the name of what was wrong with him, but it sounded really bad – like MS and Parkinson's combined, she said; only worse, because his mind went too. He was only 42 and had been a clever man – a solicitor – but had ended up in a home with people twice his age.

Her parents had split up a few years earlier before they knew how sick he really was. He'd started acting strangely – doing things that made no sense and were completely out of character. It all came to a head when, without speaking to Lori's mum, he'd loaned thousands of pounds to a friend (not even a close one), who'd agreed to repay him month by month. He never saw this so-called mate again; but it wasn't just about the money. Lori's mum was furious that he'd gone behind her back. They both turned against him for a while, but regretted it now; looking back, it was the first sign of what was to come.

"We made it right in the end," she said. "But by then, I don't know how much he was taking in. Watching him go downhill – that was the hard part. Much worse than losing him. By the time he died, he couldn't move – couldn't speak. Had to be fed through a tube." She sighed. "And that's why I'm quiet. Because it's on my mind, pretty much all the time, and – I just don't trust people. Not just because of what Dad's friend did, but.... I remember this parents' night at my old school – 3rd year I think, maybe 4th. Mum and Dad were on better terms by then – and although he was ill, he was still getting around, and his mind hadn't gone completely. Mum thought it was a bad idea, him coming along, but he insisted – I think he just wanted to keep going as long as he could.

"Anyway, a couple of my mates noticed him stagger when he walked. I tried telling them it was the illness, but they still made it into this huge joke. I got really upset at the time, but once I'd calmed down – I don't know… it's like I just can't be bothered anymore. With *anyone*."

"I get that," I said. "I was bullied in Juniors for a bit – before we lived round here. But not everyone's like those shit-for-brains, you know."

"Too many are though, Dan. And I thought they were my friends. I don't even think they *knew* it was bullying. It's just a joke, they'd say. No big deal – but it was to me. So, I gave them a wide berth, after that – and I suppose I got in the habit of keeping to myself. But now…" It was probably the first time I'd seen her smile. "I like you, Dan Cooper. And I think I could trust you – I just hope I'm right."

We only went out for a couple of months. Didn't get much past first base; not because we didn't want to, just because there was never the chance. We couldn't go back to hers, she said – her mum had really bad depression, and as well as the house being a tip, you never knew how things would be from one day to the next. So, we always ended up at mine, and there was never a time when Mum wasn't there.

Except this one afternoon, when she'd said she was working late. Our last class finished around 3.30. It was 4 when we got back – the time Mum usually got in – and we realized we'd have an hour or so to ourselves. It was all we needed. But before we could even undress, we heard the door slam.

"Only me, love! I didn't need to stay, after all."

"Shit!" We may not have started doing anything, but there was no way we could come out of the bedroom together; I'd never hear the end of it! "You stay in here," I whispered to Lori, "and I'll try and distract her." Then I ran quickly to the bathroom and flushed the bog, so Mum would think that's where I'd been…

"Are you okay?" she asked. "You don't seem yourself."

"I'm fine, Mum."

"Sure?"

"Yeah."

"You would tell me, wouldn't you?"

"Yeah."

"You and Lori haven't fallen out, have you? Because if that girl's messing you about…."

All I needed.

"Don't go on, Mum!" I snapped. "I said I'm fine – Lori's fine. Now, can you just let it go?"

"Alright – alright! No need to bite my head off!" She sighed. "Anyway- I'll just nip to the loo."

As soon as I heard the door shut, I shot back through to Lori. As I saw her out, I could tell from her face that she'd heard ever word.

Things never felt right after that – so when she ended it a week later, I can't say it was a shock. Of course, there was much more to it; but what Mum said couldn't have helped….

She was quiet as we walked home – even more so than usual – and seemed really distracted.

"Listen," I said, when she finally came out with it, "if this is because of Mum, the other week…"

She shook her head sadly. "I wish it *was* just that."

"Is it something *I've* done?"

"No! No, it's…" She tailed off. "Look, Dan, I might have the same thing as my dad."

It turned out that her dad's illness – if it wasn't bad enough – was hereditary. There was a 50% chance of Lori having the gene that caused it. Not wanting to scare her, neither of her parents had been upfront about it, but it slipped out when her Auntie Cath had visited at the weekend. And now, Lori wasn't speaking to her mum – and her mum wasn't speaking to Auntie Cath.

Lori's nan had died of the same thing, but this was years before she was born; they'd always said it was cancer.

"I could get tested for it," she said. "That would be the easiest thing – but I'm not sure I want to know, especially after seeing what Dad went through. If it's positive, it'd feel like a life-sentence – just waiting, wondering when you'd see the first signs. But one thing for sure – I'm not having kids. I just can't take the chance. And I know we've not been together long, and we're not even *thinking* that far ahead – but if things got more serious, it wouldn't be fair on you."

"I'd stand by you," I said. I'll be honest, I was struggling big-time, to get my head around it – but that much I knew.

"But would you say that a few years down the line?" she asked. "I mean, just say we stayed together – got married – and you wanted a family?"

"It wouldn't be the end of the world…"

"Things change, though, Dan. People change. And even if *you* were fine with it, your mum wouldn't be."

"But it's not up to Mum, is it?"

Lori smiled. "I don't think *she'd* see it that way."

"Then we'd have to be straight-up with her."

"No chance. That's the last thing I'd want. She doesn't like me as it is – and it's not just what she said that day. She's always in my face – like she's trying to *force* me to come out of myself – and it frustrates her. I can see it in her."

"But perhaps if she knew what's going on for you…"

"Oh, come on! We both know she'd tell you to steer clear!"

"Then I'd just have to stand my ground."

"Trouble is, Dan, she'd be right. Believe me, I wouldn't be ending it if I didn't care – but the last thing I'd want is for you to be stuck, looking after me…."

"It might not end up that way…"

"Well, Mum and Dad left it to chance, and look how *that* turned out. Sorry, Dan – I can't take the risk."

Chapter Twenty-six

Mum tried to pretend she wasn't glad but was fooling no-one. Then when Jay got with Lori, a few months later, she kept going on that I "was well rid of that girl." And as for *him*…. Perhaps she had a point where it came to Jay, but the "told-you-so" attitude really wore me down.

In fairness to him, Jay never knew how gutted I was over Lori. But talk about not letting the grass grow! And the way he used to laugh behind her back… but then – as she'd said herself – people can change…. I suppose what got me the most was that I'd thought she didn't want to be with *anyone*. I didn't doubt anything she told me about the illness – but she'd face the same problems whoever she was with, so why was it different for Jay? I'd have been there for her, if I'd had the chance. Somehow, I couldn't see Jay doing that, yet she chose *him*…

I didn't stop speaking to them, but I did take a huge step back; started hanging out more with Tim and his new crowd. Tim had been drifting away for a while; he did different classes to us and had other mates who Jay had no time for – and the feeling was mutual. Meanwhile, Rosie Darch thought we were as thick as thieves.

"Doesn't it piss you off?" she asked.

I shrugged. "Why would it?"

"Come off it, Dan! Everyone knows you're still well into Lori. And she's a nice girl – she can do way better than *that* arrogant prick!"

"So," I asked, "if you hate him so much, why does it bother you?"

"It doesn't! I'm only thinking of Lori. I just hope he doesn't hurt her, that's all – I couldn't care less about *him*!"

"All I'm saying is, for someone you don't give a shit about, you seem to talk about him a hell of a lot."

"And what would you know?" she shot back. "Just keep your nose out, okay?"

I laughed. "What - like *you* are? You're the one who brought this up, Rosie, so don't be having a go at me. It's up to you what you do. I just don't know if he's worth the effort."

"Sorry," she muttered. "I didn't mean to snap. And you're probably right."

I noticed after that she stopped going on about him – and started acting normal when he was around, instead of making a big deal of ignoring him. That seemed to throw him off-kilter – next thing, him and Lori are old news, and he's sniffing around Rosie again. I felt awful for Lori – whatever I thought of her and Jay, she didn't need this.

"I'm fine," she said, matter-of-fact, when I asked if she was alright. "Never better. So, if you've come to gloat…"

"Come on, Loz – you know me better than that."

"Well, you weren't happy about me seeing Jay, and don't try to deny it. You've barely spoken to either of us since."

"Can you blame me? I mean, from what you told me about your dad's illness… I just thought you needed time on your own, that's all."

She softened. "And I suppose you're wondering why I got with someone, after saying all that? Thing is, I *knew* it wouldn't last with Jay. That's why it was easier. And it's no problem if he's back with Rosie, because it was only ever meant to be a laugh. Never serious – not like with you."

It still got to me – my ex-girl and best mate, in front of my nose, not seeing any harm in it – but what she said made sense, and it did help me try and get past things. Or at least I would have done, if Mum had been less full-on.

It was constant. Are you okay? Are you *sure* you're okay? Stop trying to pretend, Dan, because I know you're not…why don't you just be open, instead of shutting me out? Until at last she'd gone on that much that I said, alright – so this thing with Jay and Lori *had* got me down a bit, but I was trying to move on. Then… you see! I knew it! I *knew* I was right! – and you're being so silly, son, worrying about the likes of them. And you need to try and snap out of it – after all, there's people out there with *much* worse problems. Look at poor Bill and Em…

"I'm not being funny, Mum," I said in the end, "but you always do this – keep on asking me what's wrong, then when I tell you, you have a go at me."

"I'm not *having* a go, love – I just want you to be happy."

"And I will be, if you get off my case."

"Oh, that's right! Push me away!" Then she burst into tears, and I felt like the biggest twat going.

I made her some tea. "Look, I'm sorry," I said. "I just want you to believe me when I say I'm trying to handle things, in my own way. I didn't mean to upset you."

"I know," she said, drying her eyes. "I know you didn't, love, it's just… hard at the moment, that's all. I feel so lost without Barb – and I'm trying to be strong for Bill and Em, because let's face it, it's much worse for them than it could ever be for me. And when I remember that, I feel so guilty for being upset…"

"She was your best mate, Mum," I said. "Of course it's hard."

She hugged me. "Thanks, son. You're wise beyond your years, you know that? And you're the first one to say that to me. If I try and talk to your Auntie Jan, she just looks at me as though I've grown another head! Mind you, I reckon that might be a bit of jealousy, because Barb was like the sister I'd always wanted. But even your nan and grandad – it's not that they're unsympathetic, but – I don't know…I just don't think they really understand, because Barb wasn't family. Like they're thinking, she was just a friend, and you can easily make more –

and then trying to explain that it was different with Barb; she was a one-off. I know I've still got Jean, but I hardly see her, these days, and she's having terrible trouble with Keith. Hard to believe, really – such a quiet boy… So, anyway, I can't really burden Jean and Eric at the moment, with all they've got going on.

"Of course, the one who *would* get how I'm feeling is Bill – but what that man's going through…how could I sit there, expecting him to listen to *me?* And he probably would, knowing him, but that wouldn't be right…Anyway – thanks for being here for me, love - And sorry to be such a worrywart."

Chapter Twenty-seven

Things calmed down a bit, after that – but as A-levels loomed, I knew that if I managed to get through them (which, the way I felt, I seriously doubted!), and into Uni, I'd need to get away. And by that, I meant *properly* away, not just down the road. All along, I'd set my heart on Manchester, but I could see now why that wouldn't work. Too tempting for Mum to jump on a train and turn up, interfering - all well-meant, of course, but I might as well stay at home! I'd picked Bristol as a back-up plan, if I didn't get Manchester, but now it seemed ideal; far enough from Mum, but near enough to Dad to put her mind at rest - or so I thought.

I'd never intended to cut her off - had planned to ring most nights, if need be, and come home once a month as well as in the holidays, just so she wouldn't feel pushed out. And when I told her that Sunday… don't get me wrong, I knew she wouldn't be happy, but when I mentioned staying over with Dad sometimes, I honestly thought that might help. But she sounded so jealous and bitter about it, and *that* was what got me angry; then I realized it was there all along. Since Alan, probably; maybe before that. Every time I couldn't talk to her; every time I tried, and she'd turned on me, or shut me down, or just didn't *hear* me at all.

Dad called her when I got there. I was too wound-up and needed time to get my head straight, and decided it was best to wait till I was settled in Uni. Trouble was, it took much longer to settle than I'd hoped; and I just knew that if I spoke to her, I'd be home before the first term was out. She could tell a mile off if anything was up, and there was no way I could fool her on this one. What if you're homesick? she'd asked. She was right, but I couldn't admit that. No – however lonely I was – and however much I missed her – I had to stick this out.

I was too "posh" when we lived on the estate. And now, again, I found myself on the outside – but this time, *I* was the scally! The place was heaving with hurrah-henry's; at least in my Hall, anyway, although perhaps it just seemed that way because they shouted the loudest. All from the Home Counties, privately educated – nothing down for you if you'd been to state school. "You have a very strong accent, I must say," this stuck-up cow remarked – before going on to quiz me about how bad life really was in Liverpool. How did I cope with all the crime? Was it safe to go out?

I thought loads of times about speaking to Dad, and maybe seeing if I could live with him and Sue, at least until I found my feet. But there was no way that could happen without him telling Mum – and besides, the whole point of being here was to prove I could do this on my own. The best I could do was to get my head down, focus on my work, and try and ignore the hurrah's- easy enough, but depressing as hell. After all, the social life had been the other reason to come away.

But then, about six weeks in, I got talking with this lad, Neil Hamill, from the Art class. He'd already been at Bristol for a year, on the foundation course – turned out he'd been in the same Hall I was in now and hated it just as much. Within a few months, he'd found a house-share with some others from the course, which was loads better. But now, one of his mates had found a job and dropped out, and his room was up for grabs – would I be interested? Safe to say I bit his hand off!

Neil's a good lad; a Manc, from Salford, and the first in his family to go to Uni. Always puts me in mind of a grown-up Phil – long hair, halfway down his back, loves his metal. Tough as nails, but in a good way, where he stands up for the underdog. The others in the house are sound as well; all from the same foundation course, but only Neil went on to do Fine Art. The two girls, Tammy and Jo, are doing Fashion and Textiles, and the lads – Graham, Mart and Lee – do Graphic Design. Lee's into metal, like Neil, and the others are somewhere between goth and punk. Tammy's quite posh, from Leatherhead in Surrey, but really nice with it, and nothing like those oiks in Halls. Mart's from Swindon, Graham from Sheffield; Lee and Jo, both Brummies. I just slotted in, and after a couple of days it was like I'd always been there.

The house is on a row of Georgian terraces in Clifton – a bit expensive but works out fine with six of us sharing. There's loads of bars nearby – quirky, off-the-wall places – so we usually stay local. But it's mostly house parties. It's a laugh – gets pretty wild, at times, but never out of hand, and we all look out for one another.

Within a few months of moving in, I found a Saturday job at a vintage record store, just round the corner. I love it – so much, it doesn't even feel like work. My boss, Jez Hill, seems a bit weird, and maybe slightly dodgy. A small, thin weasel of a bloke, perhaps Mum and Dad's age or slightly younger, with longish, straggly, greying-red hair, a ruddy face and bulbous "nose like God knows", as Dad calls it – which makes sense, as he seems to spend most of his time in the boozer. Although born and bred in Bristol, his family are Irish (Jez is short for Jeremiah, I think); and his thick West Country accent has a touch of Dublin drawl. I can't say I'd trust him as far as I could throw him, but he's friendly enough – mostly leaves me to get on with it. Pay's a bit crap, though, that's the only drawback – I should really ask him for a rise, seeing as I'm often left running the show while he's out on the piss, but I'll bide my time. "You're a daycent lad," he tells me – and I get loads of freebies. It could be worse.

And as for the art course, that's going brilliant – even better than I thought. It may have taken a while, and a rocky start, but I'm finally getting there.

Chapter Twenty-eight

So, you might ask – why not call Mum? After all, now things are going so well, there shouldn't be a problem. But that's just it. Life *is* going well, and I don't want that changing….

I knew how it would go. Once we'd spoken, she was sure to want to visit. There wouldn't be room in the house, so it would have to be a hotel, or with Dad and Sue. But she'd still expect to see the place – and even if we spent hours cleaning up, there was no way she'd approve. Not that it's even dirty! Everyone mucks in - only Graham needs a kick up the arse at times, but he pulls his finger out in the end. But we're pretty laid-back; and Mum, as you know, doesn't *do* laid-back! Yeah, I'll admit, it does get untidy; but in fairness, we're all trying to juggle Uni and work, and we're art students, so there's bound to be paint and stuff lying around. But Mum wouldn't see it that way. She'd take one look and freak out; and for all she learnt from Barb about Women's Lib, I reckon she'd blame the girls!

It's not just the mess, though – it's how we live – how we *are* with each other. We're all out at different times, so there's no set structure to the day. We just come and go as we please, and our mates just turn up on the spur of the moment, sometimes crashing out on the sofa. Mum *hates* that. My Grandma Nell (Dad's mum) used to have neighbours popping in and out. "I couldn't stand it!" Mum would say. Those neighbours would only stay for an hour at tops – so what would she make of us, up drinking half the night? Not to mention the parties….

They were never planned, and that's the thing I loved. They just *happened*, if enough of our mates turned up at one time – they'd mostly turn into all-nighters, yet we'd still manage to roll up for lectures or work the next day. From the sound of it, my Auntie Jan's student days were just the same, and Mum thought that was awful. "Jan was completely wild," she'd say. "Out of control."

Of course, I could never say to Mum, remember *your* younger days – because she didn't really *have* any. She married Dad within a couple of years of leaving school, then I was born, so there was never the chance. But even if there was, I get the feeling Nan expected her to be the grown-up, responsible one. I like Jan, but don't blame Mum for resenting her; I think I would have done, too.

But, at the same time, I know Mum wants me to be like *her*. I can remember being 9 or 10 – around the time she first got with Alan – and we had Nan and Grandad round for dinner.

"He's such a good lad," Nan was saying, and Mum nodded approvingly.

"I know," she smiled. "Isn't he? Doesn't give me a minute's worry."

"Like you at that age, Wend," Nan said. "You were never any trouble."

They were saying good things, but somehow, I didn't feel comfortable. It's not that I *wanted* to be trouble - but I did want to be *me*! That's what I've got here – and, as I say, I'm not ready yet to trade that in. I know she couldn't *make* me; but I could just see it ending up like it was at home. She couldn't stop me going into town, but there'd be that much debate about it that I'd never completely enjoy it – and then the Spanish Inquisition when I got back. After a while, it starts taking the shine off things, and you start to question if it's worth it.

But this *is* worth it. And I'm not saying I could do it forever; the constant partying would do my head in after a while. I've always had this side where I like quiet time, alone, and the other guys are the same – Neil and Lee especially. But, for now, I'm *loving* this life; and when it needs to end, *I'll* know when I'm ready.

Chapter Twenty-nine

Still, none of this makes me feel any less crap. She was so upset when I left, and I hate myself for that; and from what Dad tells me about her calls, I know it can only have got worse. After that talk with him, I knew it couldn't carry on like this – and I'd meant to keep my promise about speaking to her, but I hardly got a minute last week. There was always someone about, and it wouldn't have felt right calling from a phone box, especially if there's a queue. I was in the shop yesterday; Jez, as always, was down the pub by lunchtime, and the afternoon was pretty quiet. Perhaps now would be as good a time as any, I thought – but then Neil came in, and my heart dropped when I saw the look on his face.

"What is it?" I asked. "Is something up with my mum?"

All I could think of was what Dad said, about regrets – and that whatever it was, this was *my* fault, for leaving it too late. I couldn't take it in when Neil said it was Dad – after all, he was fine last time I saw him. Apart from that dodgy stomach...

"Jez," I murmured. "I'll have to let him know."

Luckily, the pub was just across the road. Neil went over to get him; they were back in minutes, Jez grumbling, Neil swearing under his breath.

"What's going on, son?" Jez slurred. "I'd only just started me pint!"

"Fuck's sake!" Neil muttered. "Is this guy for real?"

"I'll have to shoot, Jez," I said. "My dad's in hospital."

"Oh! Oh, right... okay – so, shall we close up, then? What d'you think?"

"Dunno, mate. That's your call."

"Yeah... yeah. Can you cash up before you go?"

"No," I snapped, "and I'm not being funny, Jez, but this is *your* shop. Can't you look after it, for once?"

"Now, hang on," he huffed, "no need for *that* tone."

"But it's all the time. You disappear for hours – and I wouldn't mind, but you pay me a pittance!"

"Well," sullenly, "sorry you feel that way. But, y' know, in all fairness, there's no bars on the windows…"

I laughed. "If that's your way of firing me, I'll save you the bother."

"No!" Jez panicked. "No – that's not what I meant… You know how much I think of you. Look, son, you go and see your old man, and when you're in next week, we'll talk… we'll talk…"

Neil offered to come with me to the hospital, but he works in a rock club in town, and I knew he was due in later. In truth I could have done with the moral support, but I didn't want him losing out.

"Alright," he said, "as long as you're sure. Hope all's well, brother – stay in touch."

Luckily, there was a train due when I got to Temple Meads. The journey was quick enough, but when I got there, it took ages to find where Dad was; it was mad busy (still lots of stragglers from the Friday night), and the queue for enquiries was dead-slow-and-stop. When I finally got to the ward, I found a plump, jolly-looking nurse with permed hair, and what Dad calls "Deirdre glasses"[xi]; hard to put an age to her, but maybe in her 40s, and with a strong Cardiff accent.

"Are you okay, love?" she smiled.

"Yeah," I said, "I believe my dad's in here. Brian Cooper?"

Her face seemed to drop. "Ah, yes – he's in theatre just now. Come on, lovely – I'll take you to your mam. She's in the relatives' room."

And for a minute, I thought she meant *my* mum. Ridiculous, I know – how could she have got there in that space of time? Of course, I was glad to see Sue; but just a bit gutted that Mum wasn't there with her.

Sue was on her own – Abs is at her dad's this weekend – and she burst into tears as soon as she saw me. Dad had felt rough all week, she said; he'd had that stomach-ache, which he put down to the curry last Saturday night, but it wasn't shifting. It seemed worse yesterday, and worse again this morning, but he wouldn't call the doctor – kept insisting it'd pass. He was taking ages in the bathroom, then she heard him shouting, and found him bleeding out. He'd lost consciousness in the ambulance, and they'd rushed him straight to theatre. They'd do their best, they said, but he'd lost so much blood, and it was 50-50 as to whether he'd make it.

I'd been there maybe an hour, maybe more, when Mair (the nurse I'd seen earlier) came to check on us.

"Anyone need a drink?"

Despite everything, Sue managed a smile. "A stiff gin sounds good to me! But failing that, a cuppa would be lovely. And thanks, Mair – you've been so kind."

"Least I can do." Mair chuckled. "And I wish I *could* get you the gin – I think I'd be joining you! What about you, my love?" she asked me. "Do you need anything?"

"My mum," I heard myself say. "Just my mum."

"Oh!" Mair looked at Sue, confused. "I thought *this* lady…"

"I'm Dan's step-mum," Sue explained. "His mum's in Liverpool."

"Ah – I see! I *thought* I recognized the accent!" She smiled. "Red or blue?"

"Blue-nose, through-and-through." I grinned. "Same as Dad. Mum's a red, though."

"Lots of banter, I expect?"

"Yeah – especially with my grandad!"

"I can imagine! Anyway, love – the phone's just along the corridor. I'll walk down with you."

"Look," I said, once Sue was out of earshot, "do you mind if I ask you something? Could this ulcer be my fault? It's just I've had this fall-out with my mum, and Dad's been really worried…"

Mair sighed. "You're a sensitive soul, aren't you? My son's just the same. It's a lovely way to be – but you need to watch out, because you can end up with the weight of the world on your shoulders."

"But they reckon stress causes ulcers…"

"Listen," she said, "I'm not saying that doesn't play a part, but there's usually more to it. I mean, does he like a pint? Spicy food?"

I nodded. "Yeah – loves his curries."

"Well, there you go. And I know he won't like this, but once he's back home, he'll have to stop all that – or cut back, at least."

"D' you think he *will* get home, Mair? Because Sue got told to expect the worst."

"They have to say that - there's always risks with surgery, and they'd get into a whole load of trouble if they weren't upfront. But from what Sue was saying, he's never been ill till now – so he stands as good a chance as any. I'd keep an open mind – that's all I'll say."

"I'll try, Mair – and thanks."

"No worries, love – I'll leave you to call your mam. See you later."

I hoped she was right but had this really bad feeling. Then I rang Mum and got that answerphone; and I'd never felt so lonely.

Chapter Thirty

But Mair was right. Dad did make it – although only by the skin of his teeth.

"He's one lucky man!" the surgeon said.

The "complication", it turned out, was that they'd had to remove the gallbladder. That meant the whole thing took much longer, and there was a touch-and-go moment where his heart rate dropped dangerously low. But they'd got there in the end – and it could have been a lot worse.

He didn't look as bad as I'd expected. Wiped-out, of course, but in good spirits. Smiled when he saw us.

"Dunno what happened there… Aw, come on, hon," as Sue broke down again. "I'll be fine – no harm done, eh? Besides," he winked, "someone's gotta keep you lot on your toes."

"Honestly, Bri," she sobbed, "I could bloody swing for you!" But she was laughing through her tears. "You *dare* frighten me like that again!"

"Here we go!" Dad rolled his eyes. "I might have pulled through, but I'm still not getting out of here alive!"

We only stayed half an hour. He was drifting off by then, and best to come back tomorrow, Mair said, once he's had a proper rest. I'm not sure how much he was taking in – he seemed all there one minute, totally out of it the next – but he looked happy when I told him I'd tried to contact Mum.

It was nearly midnight when we left; there was no way I'd make the last train to Bristol, so I went back with Sue. The plan was for her to drop me at the station in the morning, before going on to take a few things in for Dad, but when I woke up it was lunchtime, and she'd just that minute got home. I was out for the count, she said – and I'd looked so exhausted last night that she didn't have the heart to disturb me.

"Did you hear from Mum?" I asked. She was bound to panic when she heard the message, and I'd hoped to speak to her before she picked it up.

"Nothing this morning," Sue said, "but she could have tried while I was out. Thinking on, I'd best check the answerphone…"

Four new messages. One from Sue's sister, Helen. "Hi, hon - just called for a chat, but I'm guessing you and Bri are out for the evening. No worries – I'll catch you tomorrow."

Then one from Mair, this morning. "Hi, Sue – you may already be on your way, but just to let you know that Brian will be in for a couple more days, just to be safe and to make sure he takes things easy. He'll need to make a couple of lifestyle changes, especially when it comes to his diet, but I'll talk to you both when you come in. See you soon."

Another from Helen, around 10.30. "Sue? Only me, again – look, perhaps I'm over-reacting, but is everything okay? It's just you're normally in on a Sunday, and with not being able to get hold of you last night… Look, I'm sure I'm worrying over nothing, but when you get the chance, can you give me a ring, hon? Just to put my mind at rest!"

Then on to the last one, around midday – I'd not long missed it. "Hi, Sue – it's Wendy. I've just had a message from Dan – something about Brian being poorly, and – well, I'm hoping no news is good news, but I'm just a bit concerned. Can you let me know what's going on? I'll speak to you soon. Bye."

Sue got back to Helen straight away. "So sorry, Hel – I just wasn't thinking straight, and I was so worn-out I forgot to check the phone… Yeah, I know, such a shock… but he's okay, thank God. Men, eh? What would you do with them….?"

And now she's on to Mum. "Yes," I hear her say, "yes, Dan stayed over last night – he's here now. I'll put you on to him…"

Baby Steps

A couple of months on, and Brian's fighting fit. Not that it hasn't been hard-going, this health-kick lark, but bit-by-bit, he's getting there. Just take baby-steps, Mair told him, and you won't go far wrong. He'd doubted himself at first – especially when they gave him that diet-sheet.

"I'm not being funny, love," he said to Mair, "but are they trying to bump me off? Because I tell you now, I'll die of boredom with this!"

Mair laughed. "Look – now, bear in mind, this is strictly off-the-record. But you know that saying? A bit of what you fancy does you good? Just not all the time!" She winked. "But I never told you that…"

He tried his best with the diet, but there was only so much poached fish and plain boiled rice anyone could take – so he'd ended up tweaking the dishes he loved, to make them that bit healthier. He'd become a dab hand at what Sue called his "Scarborough Fair"[xii] roast chicken – mixed herbs, garlic and a splash of olive oil – which they're having for Sunday lunch today. It's the May Bank Holiday weekend, and tomorrow he'll use the leftovers for curry – a mildly-spiced Bhuna, to replace his usual Madras. All in moderation, Mair had said, and it seemed to have worked so far.

Abby's spending the holiday with her dad; only fair, Sue says, as she's always home for Christmas and Easter. So, in all, there's five for dinner – themselves, Dan, Wendy and her new bloke, Bill.

Touch wood, it's all gone well so far. Dan's spoken a few times to his mum on the phone, but in the eight months since he left home, this is the first time they've met face-to-face. It's almost like nothing had happened; both seem at ease and completely relaxed, which is a first for Wendy – Bill must be doing *something* right! He seems a stand-up guy; hard to believe him and the other fella were such good mates!

It's not just the May weekend they're celebrating, but Wendy's 40th, which was the day before. She and Bill are on a spa-break (perhaps *that's* why she's so chilled!), at a hotel in near the Cheddar Gorge - about half-an-hour's drive away, which Bill clearly had in mind when he booked. After lunch comes presents and a cake, which Dan helped Sue design – with a pale blue frosting, decorated in vibrant cerise. The idea came from a saying she'd had when he was a kid – "sky-blue-pink with a finny-addy border!" Wendy tears up slightly, just at the sheer amount of work that's gone into it and says she couldn't have asked for more.

They move across to the conservatory for coffee and dessert; at least Wendy and Dan, that is. Once they've left the room, Sue gives the nod to Bri and Bill, who grab their jackets and make a speedy exit to the pub, before anyone gets the chance to notice.

"Men!" Sue pretends to fume, bringing in a pot of tea and bowls of the cake, with a pot of whipped cream to help themselves. "Looks like they've snook off for a pint – wouldn't dream of asking *us* to join them! Honestly – if Bri hadn't done such a good job with dinner, I'd be calling him fit to burn! And getting your Bill into bad habits, too!"

"Well," Wendy smiles, "I'll let Bill off, seeing he's spoilt me rotten this weekend – like you all have!"

"It's only what you deserve, love. And all joking aside, Bill's a lovely fella." Sue glances at her watch. "Anyway -I'll make a start on those dishes."

They're quiet for a moment as Dan pours the tea.

"I feel awful," Wendy says, "leaving all the clearing-up to Sue."

"Well," Dan grins, "it's an unwritten rule around here – the birthday-person doesn't lift a finger! Besides, I reckon they've set it up like this."

"So we can talk?"

"Yeah – Sue will have told Dad and Bill to make themselves scarce."

She laughs. "Thought as much! And there's certainly lots to catch up on – it's knowing where to start."

They fall silent again as they finish the cake.

"Gorgeous," Wendy says. "You've done me proud, both of you. Sky-blue-pink… I'm surprised you remember that! You'd have

only been three – four at the most – and it as like a game we
had. You'd ask questions you knew the answers to, and every so
often, just to wind you up, I'd get it wrong. 'What colour's
grass?' 'Oh, *I* don't know – sky-blue-pink!' You'd go mad! '*No*,
Mummy! Everyone knows it's green!' And so serious! Woe
betide us if we laughed…And then that time you said you'd
leave home." Her face clouds. "Before you were old enough to
mean it."

He sighs. "I'm sorry, Mum. That day I went – I dunno, there
was so much crap going on in my head, and I just needed to
take a step back. I'd never meant for it to go on the way it did."

"No, love – don't be sorry. I'm the one at fault here. I've let you
down, and not just over Alan. I'd always wanted you to feel you
could talk to me, about *anything*. And you can't – because of how
I am."

"I'm just not sure how you'll react, sometimes. That's all it is.
Like that time I saw Alan in Smith's – I didn't know if you'd be
upset, or pleased we'd put things right. And in the end, it was
just easier saying nothing."

"I know," she says, "and that's what I *don't* want! You, holding
back, because I can't handle things – it's not fair on you, Dan,
and believe me, I don't *want* to be like this! And as for Alan –
I'm glad you saw him; glad he held his hand up and admitted he
was wrong. But it wasn't just about *him*, though, was it? You
needed me to listen, and all I did was rant and rave – and this is
no excuse, but it's what happens when I panic. All I could think
of was, if this leads to us breaking up, how will we manage,

and… you know what you just said now, about what's going on in your head? That happens to me, too – and if I can't see a way out, I end up blowing a fuse.

"And the thing is, Dan, I know that wasn't the first time. Years ago, when you told me about Keith Stack bullying you – I'd completely forgotten it till recently, when Jean told me how he carries on. I was shocked at first – but the more I thought about it, I remembered that day, and how upset you looked. But, as usual, I'd got myself in a state – thinking I'd need to speak to Jean, and we'd end up having this massive fall-out. You must have picked up on that, because the next thing, you said you were fibbing – but it was true, wasn't it?"

He nods. "And on the estate, too. It only stopped because of Phil. That's why we were so close."

"Oh, Dan! I knew it! And after how I was about Keith, no wonder you couldn't tell me."

"I just didn't want you stressing out."

"But that was for *me* to deal with, love. You were just a little boy – and the thought of you, carrying that around on your own…I know I can't change what's done, but if there's anything I can do to at least *try* and make it right…"

"Just keep listening, Mum - like you are now." He pauses. "And look – I was right, wasn't I – about you not liking Lori?"

"I wanted to, son, I really did. But I wouldn't call it dislike, so much as not really *knowing* her at all. I might have warmed to her if I'd just had the chance of a proper conversation."

"Remember I told you she'd lost her dad? He had this illness where you slowly waste away – mind, body, everything. And now it turns out she could have it, too."

"Sounds like Huntington's. I worked with someone years ago who had it. Really horrible disease, and even more cruel that it's hereditary. That poor, poor girl. I wish I'd known. But then," she sighs, "I guess that was another time you felt you couldn't talk to me."

"She didn't want me to, Mum. We split up when she found out. She doesn't want kids in case she's got it and said that wouldn't be fair on me – or you, in case you wanted grandkids. I said that was a long way off, anyway – and if it came to it, we could always just tell you upfront. But she thought if you knew, you'd tell me to steer clear."

"She was probably right. Does that make me a terrible person?"

"No," he smiles, "just honest."

"It's only because I'd want to see you happy – not to spend your whole life caring for someone, instead of living it to the full. It wouldn't be easy – but, you know, if she really *was* the one, I'd back you up, every step of the way. And although it's not what I'd choose for you, I'm proud of you for wanting to stand by her. Not many young lads would. Perhaps I'm wrong, but I couldn't see Jay being that loyal."

"That was never serious. It was easy with him, she said, because she knew it wouldn't last."

"Well, I suppose that does makes sense, but…I hope I'm not speaking out of turn here, but would she not think about getting tested? Just so sad to put her life on hold like that, if she turned out to be okay."

"But what if she isn't?"

"I know – it's a dreadful situation to be in. My heart goes out to her, it really does – and I feel terrible for pre-judging."

"You weren't to know."

"Look, I don't know if you're still in contact – but whatever you decide, I'm behind you."

"We've not been in touch for a while," is all he says.

He'll never forget Lori, and guesses she'll always be at the back of his mind – but in truth, he's moved on, big-time, since coming away. He went out with Julia (a friend of Nikki from the house) for a couple of months and has had several one-night stands. All very laid-back, no pressure, and everyone know the score – lads and girls alike. But would his mum understand it? Probably not – and although this is the most relaxed he's ever seen her, he's not ready to share his new life with her just yet.

"So," he asks, "are you here a few more days?"

"Just tomorrow. We're going to Bath for the day, then driving home Tuesday morning. Bill's got some jobs on Wednesday, but I'm off all week."

"Nice."

"Yeah…" Another pause, as she seems to collect her thoughts. "Listen… there's something else I need to tell you - Bill and I are engaged. We'd been planning on getting married next Spring, but we've just moved it forward to September."

"That's cool!" He laughs. "I don't know why you look so worried."

"Because there's a reason we're hurrying things up."

His smile immediately fades. "You're not ill, are you?"

"No, love – not ill…. Look, I've just found out I'm a month pregnant. It couldn't have come at a better time, for both of us – especially after all Bill's been through. I only hope you don't disapprove."

For a moment, she thinks her fears are confirmed, as he sits quietly, digesting the news. But then, to her relief, "Why would I? That's awesome, Mum! I'm made up for you… Hey, don't get upset…"

"It's just a load off my mind," she says, drying her eyes. "With us being the age we are, I… I'm probably being daft, but your nan's old neighbour, Mrs. O'Rourke, had her youngest at 42. Her older kids didn't take it well – took months for them to come round, and - well because of how things have been between us, lately… I just didn't want them going off-track again. Only you and Em know, so far – I was dreading telling her, too, but she's thrilled – oh, and I hope you don't mind her finding out first. We'd have told you together if you'd been home…"

"Mum - just chill! It's fine!"

"Good… and now I can see I've been worrying for nothing – but then, what's new?" They both laugh. "I'm better than I was, mind – and I've got Bill to thank for that. He does so much for me, but he in his eyes, it's me who's helped *him*. You're stronger than you think, he says. Perhaps he's right – but who'd have known?" She smiles wistfully. "Whoever would have known?"

THE END

References

[ii] Bowie, David. "Ziggy Stardust". 1972. RCA Records. Vinyl LP.

[iii] Chaplin, Charlie; Turner, John; Parsons, Geoffrey. "Smile". 1954. Published by Bourne.

[iv] Adams, Lee. "Put on a Happy Face". 1960. From "Bye Bye Birdie" (stage musical).

[v] Henderson, Ray; DeSylva, B.G; Brown, Lew. "(Keep Your) Sunny Side Up". 1929 Published by Ray Henderson Music Co.

[vi] Bell, Thom; Creed, Linda. "You Make Me Feel Brand New". From "Let's Put It All Together", Stylistics, 1974. Avco. Vinyl LP.

[viii] Gosh, Bobby. "A Little Bit More." From "Sitting In The Quiet", Dr. Hook, 1973. Capitol. Vinyl LP.

[ix] Lewis, C.S, "The Chronicles of Narnia", 1950-1956, published by Geoffrey Bles/The Bodley Head.
[x] Lewis, C.S, "The Lion, the Witch and the Wardrobe", 1950,

published by Geoffrey Bles.

[xi] From "Coronation Street" created by Warren, Tony, 1960. Produced by Granada Television (1960-2006); ITV Productions (2006-2009); ITV Studios (2009 to present).

[xii] "Scarborough Fair", Roud 12, Child 2; traditional English ballad.

Printed in Great Britain
by Amazon

87860146R00109